GRIMOIRES AND THE GHOSTLY GUEST

A WILLIAMS WITCH MYSTERY

BOOK SIX

ELOISE EVERHART

ALORIUM PUBLISHING

PB ISBN: 978-1-962759-05-2

Author: Eloise Everhart

Editors: Rashida Breen and Susie Driver

Cover design by GetCovers

CHAPTER 1

Spots floated in my vision as I stared down at the map of Point Pleasant that was sprawled across the couch cushions. The Retirees were talking, but I couldn't focus on their words. I stared at the point where my tracking spell had landed.

Charlie, my feline familiar, jumped up next to the map and placed his oversized white paw on the glowing motes of light that danced over the location where my daughter was. I could feel his concern through the bond. Grace was at Meredith Walker's house—the same Meredith who had cursed my family line. I fought to breathe as my chest constricted and my legs wobbled underneath me.

"Dani." Sarah grabbed me by the shoulders and yanked me around to face her. She held my gaze, her gray eyes wide. "We don't know why she's there."

I shrugged out of Sarah's grasp and bolted toward the front door. Charlie scampered after me. *Meredith has my daughter.* He yowled beside me to stop as my feet carried me to my car. The Retirees trailed after me, their voices melding together as they called my name. I threw myself into the front seat.

Betty dashed in front of my vehicle, her salt-and-pepper hair a wild mane around her head, and slapped her hands down on the hood.

"What are you doing?" I leaped out of the car.

"Making you stop." Betty glowered at me. "And think for just a minute."

I ground my teeth together. "She has my daughter."

"When has running in without a plan gone well for you?" Betty put her hands on her hips.

I faltered. She was right. *When am I going to learn that panicking isn't helpful?* I closed my eyes and steadied my breathing. "What am I supposed to do?" My voice cracked.

"First, you tell us what you saw," Betty said.

"Then we make a plan." Sarah walked around me to stand next to Betty.

A second later, Agnes joined her. "And we go in together or not at all."

They all crossed their arms and glared at me, daring me to disagree. Whenever they stood in a line together, it seemed as if they liked to line up from most to least white hair. Agnes's hair was completely white, while Betty's was a fifty-fifty mix of salt and pepper, and Sarah had one streak of silver in her otherwise-black hair. They all wore matching red track suits. Charlie joined them by giving me a disapproving glare from the hood of my car.

I sagged against the car door. "I'm still trying to make sense of it."

"Then that's even more of a reason not to run off." Betty wrapped her arm around my shoulders and led me back to the porch.

I sat down on the steps and studied my hands. The initial panic was wearing off, and exhaustion set back in. The entire evening had been emotionally draining. My boyfriend, Chris, had asked for time to think about things after I hid a murder investigation from him. *Did he break up with me?*

I pushed that thought aside and focused on the bigger problem. In 1946, Meredith Walker cursed every member of her coven, and that curse had been passed down through the generations to me, my daughter, and the Retirees. We didn't know how or why and had spent the last few months trying to figure that out. We finally succeeded and cast a spell to get a vision of what happened that night. But what I had seen left me with more questions than answers.

Sarah took a seat next to me and held my hand. "Why don't you close your eyes and tell me the first thing you saw when the vision began?"

I did as she said. Charlie jumped up next to me and head-butted me. Petting him, I replayed the vision in my head. My stomach hardened like a rock. I swallowed, my mouth dry. "I was in her living room, and there was a knock at the front door. Or at least, I think there was, because Meredith answered it."

Someone sat next to me on the other side and held my other hand. Agnes's voice came from a few inches away. Her tone was warm and caring. "Then what happened?"

"Six women pushed past her into her home. I think they were her coven. I recognized most of them from my great-grandmother's photographs." I squirmed on the step. The vision had been difficult to focus on when I first experienced it, and trying to refocus on it wasn't any easier. "I couldn't make out who said what. It was like the vision was fighting me. Everything was distorted, but I heard someone say she needed to stop. That they knew about her deal."

Betty inhaled sharply. "What deal?"

"I don't know. They said a Warden was going to come if she didn't. They threatened to strip her of her powers."

"That can't be right," Sarah said.

"After that, she attacked them." I squeezed their hands. "They put up some sort of shield around her. It was… chaotic. She kept calling them traitors. She was so angry."

The Retirees sat there silently, reassuringly, holding my hands until I could continue.

"They confined her and were trying to figure out what to do when... I don't know, something changed inside her. Her hair turned white, her eyes glowed this horrible green color, and she said something. I think it was 'May all your dreams turn to ash.' Then she attacked them again. The second before the attack landed, Beatrice, your mom, Betty, she did something. I don't know if I can explain it. It was almost like she made Meredith part of the house."

"Okay." Betty exhaled. "So she's part of the house, and your daughter is at the house. I think that would scare anyone."

"That's not what scared me." I swallowed. "Not entirely."

I opened my eyes. Betty was crouched in front of me.

"Meredith's magic looked exactly like Grace's. Or at least how Grace's looks now. Her sparkles used to be purple, but they've been turning green. Just like Meredith's were green."

Betty rocked back on her heels and almost tumbled to the ground. She caught herself at the last second and surged to her feet. For an older woman, she was still nimble. Holding her hands behind her, she paced back and forth in front of me.

"Sometimes, magic changes in appearance," Agnes said. The hopeful edge to her voice sounded forced. "Especially during a witch's developmental stage. Grace is still young."

"It can?" I grabbed on to the sliver of hope.

"It's possible." Sarah's voice rose, almost like it was a question. "But the same color? In such a short period of time?"

"It's impossible to know without investigating further," Betty said. "And the best place to start is at the source. We should go see what Grace is up to."

"And do what when we get there? Confine her like our ancestors did to Meredith?" My words came out shrill as I lost the battle against the panic bubbling inside me.

Charlie shoved himself onto my lap and nestled his head against my neck, purring gently into my ear.

Sarah interjected, "No. Repeating history is foolish. We should..."

"Figure it out when we get there?" Agnes stood. "There are too many unknowns for us to make a plan. Let's do recon. And if things get tense, at least all of us can access our magic right now."

All our curses had manifested differently. For Grace and me, the Williams line, we had no control over when or how our powers of divination activated, which was stressful on the psyche. Agnes's curse prevented her from ever leaving Point Pleasant. She was stuck on Whidbey Island, never able to even visit Seattle, which wasn't far away. Betty's magic always had unintended and often negative side effects. And Sarah could only access her magic during the full moon. I glanced up at the sky. Clouds covered the full moon. If it was going to be a confrontation, now was the best time.

Charlie leaped off my lap as I stood. He stared up at me, trust in his eyes. I squatted down to pet him. "This might be a bit too dangerous for you, buddy. Do you mind staying home?"

He growled and turned back to the house, his tail swishing angrily behind him. I let him back inside then walked toward my car. The Retirees scurried after me. Betty power walked until she was ahead of me by a few paces. She closed my car door and continued to her truck. "I'll drive."

I opened my mouth to object but closed it without saying anything. The panic was still bubbling under the surface. It wouldn't take much for me to become reckless again, so it was a good idea to have someone with a clear head driving. I hugged my arms to my body and followed Betty to her truck.

No one said a word as we drove through town. We followed the roads into one of the older neighborhoods, which was filled with post–World War II construction, and pulled to a stop half a block from Meredith Walker's house. The night was quiet, and most of the houses on the street were dark. Sitting across the street from Meredith's house was Grace's car. In the dim light, I could make out her shape sitting on the hood. My eyes flicked between her back and the house.

Meredith Walker's house was the creepiest building on the block. The Wardens of the West had placed an illusion over the building to make it look like an abandoned home, with a touch of magic that scared people away. It was an eyesore that no one would ever want to approach or do anything about. Under the spell, it was a well-preserved time capsule. The home hadn't been occupied since that fateful night.

I inhaled through my nose and exhaled through my mouth as I tried to calm my nerves. It was so quiet—too quiet. I exchanged glances with the Retirees. They gripped each other's hands, their eyes full of apprehension. It was the moment of truth. And the truth had the potential to be very scary. None of us wanted something to be wrong with Grace, but I also couldn't imagine any of us thinking something wasn't wrong with her either. It was the degree of wrong that we were there to figure out.

Squaring my shoulders, I flung the passenger door open and climbed out of the truck. Before my confidence faltered, I strode down the road toward my daughter. With each step, I scrambled to figure out what to say when I reached her. I came to a stop next to her car, and every option fled my mind as she looked up at me, her eyes red rimmed.

"Mom?" Grace cried. "How did you know I would be here?"

"I..." I stared into her eyes. *What if the color change doesn't mean anything?* "I was worried about you when you didn't show up for the witches' school lesson."

Grace nodded and wiped at her eyes. She glanced at the

Retirees as they fanned out behind me. "I'm sorry. I know I should have been there. It's just I… I couldn't bear it if the spell failed. I'm used to not knowing what happened. But the thought of never figuring it out… of being stuck with our curse forever, I couldn't face that."

"Oh, sweetie." My heart broke as she slipped off the car hood and collapsed into my arms. I patted her back, careful not to touch any of her exposed skin. Grace's psychometry abilities were incredibly strong. She could pick up the emotional residue from any object or person with a touch, and it frequently overwhelmed her as it created vicious feedback loops. I didn't want her to feel my fear, not when it was clear she was already feeling so lost herself.

"Did you guys do it already?" Grace whispered into my shoulder.

I nodded. "I'm still trying to make sense of it, to be honest."

"What did you see?" Grace pulled back. She pulled her sweater down to cover her hands.

My eyes flicked between them and her face. She wasn't wearing gloves. For the past few months, she barely took them off because they helped protect her from an overly emotional world. *Why isn't she wearing them?* The pressure in the back of my head began to build. There was something important about her missing gloves. My heart skipped a beat. *What had she touched when she hugged me? Was she checking to see how I felt?* I didn't know what to think. I didn't know if I could trust my daughter.

I forced a sad, sympathetic smile onto my face. I had practiced the expression and perfected it over all my years as a claims adjuster. Frequently, when people were meeting me during the claims process, it was on one of the worst days of their lives. A sympathetic smile went a long way to make them feel understood and seen. "I saw Meredith Walker in her living room, and her coven arrived. I think I'm going to have to sleep on it to figure out what else happened, because it was very distorted."

Her expression fell, and she hugged her arms to her body. "I was really hoping you would have seen more."

I chewed on my lip. *She seems normal. What if the sparkle color doesn't mean anything? I could be overreacting for no reason.* I couldn't be sure, and as my gran always said, better safe than sorry. "Me too. But I might understand more of it after a good night's sleep."

"Are we good to go, then?" Agnes sidled up next to me and tried to catch my eye.

"Yeah..." I glanced between the Retirees and Grace. "I think we all need to rest, and we can figure out what to do in the morning."

"Did you need a ride home, Mom?" Grace asked.

I glanced back at Betty's truck. I didn't have a good excuse not to get a ride from my daughter. We were going to the same place. I nodded. "Let me just check the truck to make sure I've got all my stuff."

The Retirees drifted off to the truck, while Grace opened up her car door and took the driver's seat. I followed Betty and climbed in. I stared at Grace's car. It was too far for her to listen in without using magic, and there were no sparkles coming from her vehicle.

"What do you want to do?" Sarah whispered, her eyes flicking from me to the car.

"I don't know. She seemed like herself."

"She did. But you never know what Meredith's ghost, if that's what she even is, did to her. Why come here?" Agnes fidgeted in her seat.

Betty grabbed my hand. "There is something wrong. I can feel it."

I nodded. The hairs on the back of my neck hadn't gone down through my entire conversation with Grace. "Don't worry. I'm calm now. I won't do anything reckless."

Agnes grabbed her purse from the floorboards and fished around inside it. "Do you still have your protection amulet I made you?"

"Yes." I retrieved it from the inside pocket of my bag. "Just in case we ever had to go back into Meredith's house."

Agnes held up a small vial. "Put it on, and if anything seems off, anything at all, I want you to drink this."

I wrinkled my nose. It was one of the tinctures we had made that helped protect against mind-altering magic. The things tasted awful. I took it from her and shoved it into my pocket. "I promise."

I had been in the truck long enough, so I put on the amulet and scooted toward the door.

Betty grabbed my arm before I got out. "We need to talk about what to do. Meet us tomorrow for brunch at Slice of Life."

I nodded and hopped out of the truck, then I lowered my head and marched back to Grace's vehicle. A weight had settled over my shoulders. I didn't know if it was possible for this week to get any worse. I climbed into her car and put on my seat belt.

"I love you, Mom." Grace started her engine and pulled away from the curb.

The pressure at the back of my head pulsed. My Sight was desperately trying to tell me something. Betty had been right. Something was wrong with Grace. But I couldn't put my finger on what it was. She looked and sounded right. I studied her out of the corner of my eye as I clutched the vial Agnes had given me in my pocket. Grace had put her gloves back on. She never took them off, not if she could help it. *Why wasn't she wearing them when we arrived?* I swallowed.

"I love you too," I said.

CHAPTER 2

Time seemed to crawl all morning. Each second stretched until five minutes felt like an hour. I focused as much as I could on the task at hand. The photos I'd taken during my last home inspection weren't going to label themselves. After each photo, my eyes flicked to the clock. Brunch time couldn't come nearly fast enough. *Why couldn't the Retirees have said to meet them for breakfast?* I fidgeted in my seat until exactly ten fifty a.m., when I stood from my desk, grabbed my purse, and marched out of my office.

My feet carried me to the Slice of Life diner. I had walked there so many times over the past year that my body knew the way without my having to think about it. Instead, my brain replayed every second of the night before on repeat. My heart ached as it looped back around to the moment Chris had said he needed time to think. My bad luck had started at that moment, and the whole night went downhill from there. I tried to distract myself by studying the new spray-painted murals that were going up all over town. The mysterious artist had started on Madison Street on the building that used to be Abby's bistro, Eats and Treats, and had spread from there. They were beautiful. But even they couldn't keep my mind off the creeping dread that had been building in the back of my mind all night.

I stepped into the diner. Only a quarter of the tables were filled. Since it was the beginning of brunch, I arrived during the small lull between the end of the breakfast rush and before the lunch surge began. Seated in the middle of the room were the Retirees. Every quarter, Willow rearranged the decorations on the walls. She had photos and artwork of the town going back to its founding. This quarter, she had the diner divided into the four seasons. The Retirees had claimed a spot in the spring section, which boasted photos of downtown in full bloom.

Each of the Retirees had a slice of pie, untouched, sitting in front of them. My stomach rumbled. It was close to my usual lunch anyway, and the scent of spiced apples filled the air. I nodded at the Retirees and stopped by the counter to put in an order. Willow and Abby stood at the register, engrossed in a deep conversation about the merits and flaws of gas ovens. They stopped as I approached.

It felt odd seeing Abby behind the counter. After her bistro had been vandalized, she had lost her lease at Eats and Treats. Willow was kind enough to give her a spot to cook in her kitchen so she could start up her food truck again until she found a new space. She already looked at home here, chatting away with her "archrival." They looked at ease standing next to each other—Willow with her long strawberry-blond hair piled high on her head in a messy bun, her usual red-framed glasses, and her flowing bohemian-style dress, and Abby with her short brown pixie cut, black slacks, and polo shirt.

Despite my hunger, my brain couldn't focus on the menu. I swallowed and stared up at the photos of food.

"Want us to surprise you?" Abby asked.

I nodded.

"Coming right up," Willow said.

They bowed their heads together and began whispering back and forth as I retreated from the counter and made my way to the Retirees.

I took a seat next to Sarah. "Am I glad to see you guys. I've been frazzled all day."

Sarah touched my arm and held up a finger for me to wait.

Agnes grabbed the salt shaker from the table and poured a small pile of it into the center of her palm. When she murmured over it, the air in front of her shimmered with an iridescent quality. It shifted from teal to purple to blue and back again as she cast a spell. I was so glad only other witches could see the lights we gave off when casting magic. No one else in the diner would notice the strange quality around our table. Once she was done, she sprinkled the salt in a barely noticeable circle around the table.

"A spell to prevent eavesdropping," Agnes said. "I added something to it that will alert me if anyone tries to listen in."

My heart clenched. It was to protect us from Grace. My daughter knew how to track and to spy on distant locations with a scrying spell. I hated that it might be necessary. But none of us knew what the change in appearance of her magic meant, and we couldn't take any chances.

"What happened after we left last night?" Betty asked.

"Not much that I could tell. Grace took me home. We both went to bed. Charlie knew something was wrong, so he stayed up all night, watching my bedroom door." Through my bond to my familiar, I could sense that he was finally sleeping. He had been exhausted when I left that morning and hadn't been pleased when I left him behind, but I wanted him to keep an eye on Grace—as much as he could anyway.

"Where is Grace now?" Agnes asked.

"Still at home, I think." I fidgeted in my seat. "She was still in bed when I left this morning. And Charlie hasn't noticed her leave."

"All right." Betty leaned forward, her hands splayed across the table. "What do you want to do?"

"I..." My mind went blank. *What are we supposed to do? She's my daughter.* "I thought you guys would know."

"We..." Betty's mouth opened and closed as she struggled to find the words.

Agnes put her hand on Betty's arm. "We've never dealt with something like this before."

"Okay. So we're basically going in blind." I lowered my gaze and studied my hands as I clasped them in front of me. We were all in unfamiliar territory. While the situation was nothing like handling insurance claims, my life as an adjuster was the only thing I really had to pull on. Whenever I encountered something I had never come across before, the first step was always the same. "Step one is to find out more information."

"I think we should start—" Betty stopped talking as Willow appeared at the side of the table with a plate of food.

"You looked like you could use some comfort food." Willow held out the plate for my inspection. "I made the bacon mac 'n' cheese. Abby made the roasted brussels sprouts, also with bacon and cheese."

My stomach rumbled as she sat the plate down in front of me. It smelled divine. "Thank you."

Willow beamed. "I know it's only been a day, but it's been a blast having Abby here already. We've been teaching each other tips and tricks all morning."

"I'm glad it's working out," I said.

"Oh, and Abby said to tell you it's on the house." Willow took a step back from the table and scurried away before I could object.

I took a bite. The mac 'n' cheese had a sharp bite to it. I groaned. It had been made out of Beecher's cheese, which was a local cheese company. They made the best sharp white cheddar I'd ever had.

The Retirees only waited for me to take a few bites before they started tittering. They had a habit of talking over one another. Somehow, they understood what they were saying, but it was impossible for me to track.

I shoved a few more bites into my mouth before I cut in. "Where should we begin?"

The Retirees glared at one another. Sarah slouched into her seat, crossing her arms over her chest. Agnes threw up her hands and followed suit. Betty grinned. Whatever argument they had been having, she had won, as usual.

"We should—"

The pressure in my head spiked as my phone rang. I gasped and doubled over. Spots formed in my vision. With each ring, the pain surged through my skull. I swayed in my seat, struggling to keep upright.

Agnes scrambled to her feet. Her chair wobbled behind her as she darted around the table to my side. Betty stood, leaned over the table, and peered into my face.

"Dani, are you all right?" Sarah's hand hovered over my arm. "What's happening?"

"I don't know." I grimaced and slumped forward as the call went to voicemail. My head throbbed.

Sometimes, when my Sight, my witch's power that let me peek into the future, wanted me to pay attention to something, the pressure in the back of my head went up. It was a low-level headache that, while annoying, had never really hurt before. At least, not as far as I could remember. This felt like a siren had gone off in my head. My hands shook as I fished my phone out of my bag. I almost dropped it as it chimed when a text message came in, and another spike of pain stabbed through my head.

> **HEATHER:**
> One of my guests was murdered.
>
> Please come. I need you.

"I've got to go." I shoved my phone into my bag and surged to my feet.

"Wow." Betty grabbed me. "Are you sure you should be going anywhere? You don't look so good."

My phone chimed again in my pocket. Spots flooded my vision, obscuring most of the room from view. "I don't think I have a choice."

"We didn't finish talking about Grace," Agnes mumbled.

I shrugged out of Betty's grasp and bobbled toward the front door.

"We need to search her room," Betty said.

I froze in place. I couldn't stay, but I also couldn't leave after Betty had said something like that. If we did that and Grace found out, she would lose trust in me. It had been hard to build it back up after I had divorced her father, moved away, and hidden our witch ancestry from her. *Can I risk that?*

"There might be clues to what she's been up to in there," Sarah said.

They were right. If Grace was up to no good, there might be something in her room. That was the best place to start.

My phone chimed again, and a queasy feeling filled my stomach. My Sight was being more impatient than normal. It was almost like it had a mind of its own and wanted me to go to the bed-and-breakfast now, not later.

"Okay. I'll call you when she's out of the house."

I stumbled out of the diner without giving the Retirees a second look and jogged the few blocks to the Bizzy Bean. With every step, the pressure in my head pulsed as if it were telling me to keep going, to get there faster. Whatever was waiting for me there was important.

CHAPTER 3

My pace slowed as I approached Bee's Bed-and-Breakfast. It was in the same row of brownstones as Heather's Bizzy Bean Café. Heather had recently taken over management of it when her mother had fallen and broken her leg, so she now owned or managed everything on the strip. The bed-and-breakfast occupied the townhomes on either side of the café, with apartments over the café that connected both sides of it. Iris, Heather's mom, had lived in one and Heather in the other. She was now the only one who lived above the café.

My heart sank as I approached the building. I had expected Victor's van. He was the only medical examiner in town, after all. But parked next to the van was Chris's cruiser. There weren't many options from the sheriff's department to respond, but after how we'd left things during our last conversation, facing Sheriff Bob Wright would have been preferable, and Bob wasn't exactly a fan of mine.

I lingered outside the front doors of the bed-and-breakfast, my eyes on Chris's car. The pulsing in my head grew stronger the longer I dallied, so I pulled the door open and shuffled inside. I followed the sound of voices past the foyer and up the stairs to the second floor. Clustered in the hallway outside an open door were Heather, Chris, and an unexpected face: Izzy's, a local reporter who had helped me in the past.

She hovered about a foot away from Heather. Her hair had changed colors again. It was a pastel pink and hung in choppy waves around her face. She wore a loose red silk blouse that fell past her hips, black leggings, and little black booties.

They all glanced at me as I stepped onto the landing. Heather's bright-red hair hung limply around her shoulders. Her oversize sweater made her look small as she dabbed at her eyes with a tissue. My heart fluttered at the sight of Chris dressed in his usual deputy's uniform. He had his hand on Heather's shoulder, his brown eyes misting with concern. He tensed when he noticed me staring.

I swallowed and took a faltering step forward, and Chris turned away, motioning for Izzy to follow him into a room farther down the hall. My mouth went dry as he strode away. He had only just told me the previous night that he needed space to think about us. He wasn't sure if I liked him or his access to case files. Knowing that he didn't trust me broke my heart. And I was sure seeing me here so soon, especially at another crime scene, wasn't making it easier for him to figure out what he wanted.

The pressure in my head spiked again, so I darted forward before it had a chance to build.

Heather stood with her back to the open door. She sniffled as I stepped up next to her and pulled her into a hug. I peered over her shoulder. Only about a third of the room was visible from my vantage point. I could make out a corner of the bed and half of Victor's shoulder. He was crouched on the far side of the room. And next to him, poking out from behind the bed, was a woman's foot wearing a white tennis shoe.

"Do you know who she is?" I asked Heather.

She nodded into my shoulder. "Linda. I thought it was a guest, but it wasn't. She wouldn't have been here if I hadn't begged her to come in to work today."

Linda had worked as an intern for Heather over the winter break. When Heather had unexpectedly needed to take over the bed-and-breakfast, Heather asked her to return. I patted Heather's back. It wasn't her fault, but she had such a tender heart that I couldn't imagine her not beating herself up over it. "I'm so sorry."

As a shiver went down my spine, the hairs on my arms stood up. I shuddered as the pressure in the back of my head pulsed again.

Heather pulled back and peered into my face. "Did you sense something weird?"

I nodded.

"I knew it." Heather squeezed my hand. "It's like you're meant to do this. Linda was a good person, and she deserves to have the best people investigating."

Izzy and Chris stepped out into the hall. He handed a business card to her. "If you think of anything, please call."

She nodded and stared at the card.

"Miss Bellerose?" Chris motioned Heather over.

Heather gave him a quizzical look. He was rarely so formal. I squeezed her hand back, and she walked down the hall toward him. Heather followed him as he stepped back into the other room.

I glanced between Izzy and the open doorway. The body bag had been lifted onto a gurney, and Victor was writing something on a clipboard. I stepped into the room to discover that he wasn't alone.

Harrison Abbott, despite his impressive height, had been hidden by the door. His deputy uniform seemed oversize on his thin frame. He smiled sheepishly at me. "I don't think you're supposed to be in here, Dani."

"Sorry." I held up my hands and stepped back out into the

hall. "I'm just worried about Heather. Do you have any idea what happened to Linda?"

Victor put down the clipboard and turned toward me. His white hair was styled into a sleek pompadour, and his neatly trimmed beard was perfectly lined up with his intricate regency collar. Victor had always been a little eccentric, but it was part of what the town loved about him. He gave me a gentle smile. He was used to me asking questions, and because I had gained his trust, he was also used to answering them when he probably shouldn't. "I'll know for sure once I've done the autopsy. Right now, I can't tell if it was strangulation or the blow to the head that did it. We're almost done here, but if you could give Heather my condolences, I would appreciate it."

"Of course."

Victor grabbed the end of the gurney, and Harrison stepped up to hold the other end. I backed up to give them space as they carried Linda away and stared at their backs as they disappeared down the stairs.

Silence filled the hallway, and I glanced behind me. Izzy was still staring blankly down at the card in her hands, a slight tremor in her fingers. The pressure at the back of my head continued to pulse, so I gritted my teeth and stepped back into the bedroom where Linda had been killed. The second I crossed the threshold, I shuddered. The hair on the back of my neck bristled. I took a tentative step forward.

The room overlooked the courtyard in the back. It was winter, so the large maple tree was bare of leaves. The room was comfortable looking. A queen-size bed took up the center of the room, with an impressive solid-wood headboard against the right wall. It had flowers carved into it in a spiraling pattern. The flower theme continued throughout the room—into the bedspread, the artwork, and the small cushions on the recliner in the corner. The pressure in my head abated, and the hair on my arms finally went down. My

Sight was no longer screaming at me to do something. I exhaled, my shoulders dropping from their tense position.

"Did someone leave the window open?"

I jumped at the sound of Izzy's voice behind me and spun around toward her. She stood in the doorway, hugging her arms to her body.

"It's cold in here," Izzy continued. "I'm going to go grab a sweater and a cup of coffee. Did you want one?"

I blinked and nodded. The pressure at the back of my head returned as she backed out of the room. The thought of following her made the pressure spike. I winced and turned back around. Apparently, a coffee break was not in the cards today. My Sight was being more demanding than usual. *Is it being caused by the curse? My powers aren't always reliable, but this is a whole new level.*

The tension was creeping back into my neck, and I shrugged to loosen my shoulders. I glanced back at the doorway. The hallway was empty. I didn't know how long I had to look around. I closed my eyes and murmured the words to the spell that would heighten my senses. The golden light of my magic glowed through my eyelids. As the last word of the spell left my lips, all of my senses went into overdrive.

The pain in my neck from the tense muscles throbbed. Even with my eyes closed, the brightness from the sun streaming in through the window hurt. The shrill sound of seagulls out by the pier pierced the air. Down the hall, Heather was giving her statement. I shut down the senses I didn't need so I could focus better, until only my vision was still sharp, and opened my eyes.

To the naked eye, the room had appeared clean. But now, every little speck of dust hanging in the air stood out. I spun in place, taking in as many details as I could. Victor had mentioned a head wound, but there was no blood anywhere. I darted over to the bed and peeked at where Linda had been lying. There was a small amount of it on the floor, but it was a small pool and appeared tacky. Chewing on my lip, I studied the ground where she had been lying. The fibers of the carpet seemed different.

I took a step back and stared at it. The room had recently been vacuumed, and the carpet fibers were all pushed in a uniform line across the room in most places, except for a line about two feet wide leading from the door to next to the bed. *Is that where Victor carried her out?* The gurney had wheels, so it wouldn't have flattened it out in such an even line.

I crouched and lowered my head to the floor so I could study it from the side. Down there, I could see the lines where the gurney had traveled. And the trail of bent-over fibers was even more pronounced. Something had been dragged. *Or someone? There's no blood, so maybe she was moved here.*

"This is a crime scene, Miss Williams." Bob stepped into the doorway.

I scrambled to my feet and dropped the spell.

He stood there in his sheriff's uniform, with his hands behind his back, glowering at me, his dark-blue eyes cold. "Out. Now." He stepped back from the door and pointed down the hallway. "Before I cart you in for interfering with a police investigation."

I darted out of the room. The commotion had attracted attention. Heather and Chris peered at me from the end of the hall, and standing on the stairs leading up to the third floor were the other guests. They gawked at me. My face flushed as I scampered toward the exit. I glanced back down the hall. Chris had turned away, and Heather gave me an apologetic wince. Bowing my head, I retreated down the stairs.

My face was still flushed when I got to the foot of the steps. Bob was not my biggest fan. That, I was used to. But the cold shoulder from Chris hurt. And having all those strangers see me kicked out of a crime scene was just embarrassing. I stepped to the side to clear my head.

A few minutes later, Heather joined me. "Are you all right?"

"Yes." I sighed. "No. Chris asked for time to think last night."

Heather leaned against the wall next to me and held my hand. "Is it because of the Abby thing?"

I nodded. After Abby's bistro had been vandalized and a dead body found inside, she had become a person of interest when the only prints on the murder weapon were hers. I had helped Abby by keeping her location a secret while I investigated. Chris wasn't sure if he could forgive me for that. But it had felt like the right decision at the time. Even in hindsight, it felt like the right decision. Abby was innocent.

"Maybe you should tell him what you are," Heather said. Ever since I had come clean to Heather about being a witch, our friendship had become even stronger. But I didn't know if Chris would react the same way.

Izzy stepped out of the café next door with two coffees in hand, saving me from responding. She walked over to us and handed me a cup.

"Thank you." I sipped tentatively at the coffee.

"I want to work with you on the case," Izzy said.

I almost spit out the coffee. "What?"

"I'm not naive. While I might be stuck writing the entertainment section, I'm still a journalist. I know how to ask the hard questions." Izzy squinted at me. "I know you wouldn't be here if you weren't investigating. I want in."

I wiped my mouth. "I don't know. I—"

"I'm the one who found the body. And I don't think I'll sleep well until I know whoever killed that girl has been brought to justice." Izzy held my gaze as she stepped in front of me.

My eyes flicked between Heather and Izzy. They were

both staring at me, waiting for me to respond. My heart sank. I wasn't sure if I had the brain space available to investigate. I had Grace to focus on. And I didn't want to alienate Chris any more than I already had. I chewed on my lip. *I don't think I can.*

The stabbing pain at the back of my head, which had subsided when I entered the bedroom, came back full force. A gasp escaped my lips, and I closed my eyes to block out the floating spots that had filled my vision. Even with my eyes closed, I could still see them. *Or maybe I can't say no.* I exhaled, my breath shaky.

"Are you okay?" Heather put her hand on my shoulder.

"Migraine." I winced. "Yes, I'll do it."

"And you'll let me help?" Izzy asked.

I nodded.

The pain vanished in an instant, like I had tapped out of a wrestling match and been released. I would have to talk to the Retirees about it to see how my grandmother had dealt with the headaches when our powers tried to dictate our lives.

I opened my eyes, and Izzy thrust her hand out toward me. We shook.

"All right, I've already started working on a list of potential witnesses. We just need to figure out how to persuade the other guests to talk to us." Izzy pulled out her phone and started tapping. "I might be able to convince my editor to let me write another crime piece, but he's been moody lately, so I'm not sure if I can pull that off."

"I can help," Heather said. "They all love my coffee. I'm sure I can entice them to talk to you guys by offering a free cup."

"If Bob catches us, he'll cart me off. I'm sure of it," I said.

"I'll call you as soon as he leaves, then." Heather had a determined glint in her eye.

We made plans for Izzy and me to come back to interview the guests the next morning then disbanded. I put my hands in my pockets and trudged back to my office. The problems I had to deal with were mounting minute by minute. I felt like I was trying to juggle, and someone had just thrown in a fourth ball. Keeping three in the air was hard enough. I didn't think I had time to handle more than family, work, and the curse—but I didn't have a choice in the matter. I had to investigate the murder, or my headaches caused by my curse would debilitate me. The pain could make me either drop the other balls or, worse, end up in the hospital.

CHAPTER 4

That night, I couldn't sleep, and I went into work early. I spent the morning fidgeting at my desk. Focusing on the work the day before had been bad enough. Now that I had the added stress of a murder investigation on my plate, it was almost impossible to get anything done. By the time Heather texted me at eight thirty, I had checked my phone at least a hundred times. I didn't know why I even bothered, because the second the text came through, the pressure in my head spiked. I couldn't have missed or ignored the text even if I wanted to.

I quickly packed my bag and darted into the foyer. The light in the Pleasant View Insurance Agency across the hall had turned on while I worked. The closed office door muffled the sound of Olivia's heels clicking on the wooden floors. She was just settling in for the day. I ducked my head and darted for the front door. While she was a great conversationalist, I didn't have time to be social that morning.

Since the Bizzy Bean was only a few blocks from my office, I left my car parked outside my building and power walked to the café. While Heather was sure Bob hadn't returned to the crime scene, I didn't want to risk his noticing my car parked right outside it if he decided to drive through town for something. With every murder I helped solve, he liked me less and less. I didn't think it was possible for him to dislike me more than he had after the first, but now, his disdain was so strong he had almost a visceral reaction to seeing me when I popped up near an investigation.

I slowed my pace as I approached the café. Overnight, another mural had gone up. It was on the vintage bus stop across the street. Heather was in the midst of preparing for a new window display. Last month's artwork had been scraped from the glass, and it was currently bare, waiting to be repainted that evening. It was always strange seeing the windows empty. For one day a month, they were clear of paint, and every other day, they were filled with images of cats playing with bees. I was staring so hard at the blank window that I almost walked straight into a man on the street.

"Excuse me, ma'am," he said.

"Sorry," I replied as I stepped to the side. I glanced at him. He was young and had a clipboard in hand.

"Do you have a moment to talk about—"

I ducked my head and darted past him into the café. I didn't know what cause he was collecting signatures for, but I didn't want to miss my opportunity to interview the bed-and-breakfast guests.

Warm air enveloped me as I stepped inside. I shrugged out of my jacket and walked into the plexiglass cat enclosure on the left-hand side to meet up with Heather and Izzy. They were already seated at a booth in the back.

"Which two are coming down?" Izzy asked.

"Mason Grant and Stacey Holmes." Heather read their names off her phone. "They had the rooms up on the third floor. The guy on the first floor wasn't in his room when I went by, so I wasn't able to bribe him with free coffee and scones."

I slid into the booth next to Izzy. "What do you know about them?"

"Not a lot. I've been so busy running the café and the bed-and-breakfast that I haven't had time to chat with them much." Heather sagged into her seat. "I think Mason said he was in town looking for some property to buy or something like that. He's some sort of real estate developer. And Stacey is a widow. I can't remember if she said she was here to commemorate her late husband's birthday or their anniversary. He apparently loved bed-and-breakfasts, so she visits a new one every year."

"And what about Linda? Do you know much about her?" Izzy pulled out a notepad from her pocket and jotted down the names of the guests.

"She was going to the University of Washington, studying business. I know she wanted to get into the hospitality industry." Heather teared up. "She liked cats and was really good at crossword puzzles. In the few weeks she was here, she always beat me to finishing the puzzle in Sunday's paper."

I squeezed Heather's hand. "She sounds lovely."

"She wouldn't have been here if I hadn't begged her to come back after the internship program ended." Heather sniffed and wiped her nose with a napkin. "Poor Chris had to do the notification to her family yesterday. I don't know how he can handle doing that."

"When are the guests going to be here?" Izzy asked gently.

Heather glanced at the clock above the door. "About fifteen minutes."

"All right." I pulled out my phone. "I think we should do a little bit of snooping on social media before they get here. I'll start with Linda. Izzy, could you look into Stacey? And, Heather, can you take Mason?"

They nodded and grabbed their phones.

Linda was the same age as Grace. My heart clenched. The news of her death was already out. There were almost a hundred posts already, expressing disbelief and condolences to her family. I scrolled through them until I found ones from Linda herself. She was a prolific poster. It didn't look like she kept much of her life private. There was photo after photo, documenting everything from what she ate to who she spent time with. I mentally noted repeat names. There were a lot. She was a member of a sorority and seemed to help out with almost every event on their social calendar. One name repeated more often than the rest, though: Alyssa Warren. They had been friends since kindergarten.

I glanced at the time. We only had a few more minutes. I put down my phone. "What did you guys find?"

"Mason is a real estate developer, like I thought. I found his business website. Looks like he does residential work, mostly. It's all photos of beautiful homes," Heather said.

"Stacey is a colorful lady. She's in an intense flame war with her neighbor, Kathy, over casserole recipes." Izzy continued scrolling, her eyes getting wider by the second. "Apparently, Kathy stole her recipe and posted it online in her food blog without Stacey's permission."

"A flame war over a casserole?" I chuckled.

"That's the most recent one," Izzy said. "She's also been in arguments over appropriate parking etiquette, the temperature of the coffee at her community center, and what time of year you can barbecue in your own yard."

"She sounds... interesting." Heather's voice rose on the last word, like it was a question. "How about you, Dani? What did you find?"

I scrolled back through the posts. "Linda's a local girl who's had the same best friend since kindergarten. It looks like they joined the same sorority. I was thinking about messaging her to extend my condolences and maybe offer some sort of care package for the sorority sisters."

"You can say it's from the Bizzy Bean if you want to," Heather said.

"That'll make things easier." I pecked out a message to Alyssa. "I found her mom's information too. Mind if I make a similar offer?"

"Go ahead."

The front door opened, letting in a cold breeze. A man and a woman entered. I vaguely recognized them from the bed-and-breakfast that morning. They had stood on the stairs, staring at me, as Bob kicked me out of the crime scene. My face flushed at the memory. I quickly typed a second message to Linda's mother then tucked my phone into my pocket as they approached the table.

Stacey was maybe an inch over five feet. Her short, curly brown hair was styled into a cute bob. She wore a simple A-line dress that fit her full-figured body perfectly. Her distinct smile lines gave me the impression of someone who lived with gusto. Mason, on the other hand, wore a well-tailored navy-blue suit that looked custom made. His diamond-studded cuff links caught the light as he fiddled with his sleeves. He had a well-polished image. Something about the stark black of his hair, an obvious dye job, made me think he worked hard to exude a successful image. It was slicked back, accentuating his widow's peak. The only thing warm or inviting about him was his brown eyes.

Heather stood and motioned them over. Stacey took the lead and claimed the last remaining seat in the booth. Mason grabbed a chair from a nearby table and scooted it over.

"Thank you so much for agreeing to come down." Heather inched out of the booth around Mason's chair. "I really appreciate how understanding you both have been with all the disruptions on the second floor today. I'll be right back with your complimentary drink and scone." She scurried away from the table.

Stacey stared after her for a second before turning back to me with a mischievous glint in her eye. "Have you known Ms. Bellerose long?"

"Yes," I said. "We've been friends for years."

Stacey's eyes traveled to Izzy, her eyebrow cocked, waiting for her answer.

Izzy shrugged. "Not particularly. I'm just here for the free coffee."

I eyed Izzy. While she might not have known Heather well, it wasn't like they had just met. They'd interacted with each other a few times over the past few months—especially during the investigation into Edmund Hastings's death not too long ago. *Why is she feigning ignorance?*

"It's an awful business." Stacey sighed dramatically. "It must have been terrible for you this morning. You're the one who found that poor maid, aren't you?"

Izzy nodded. "I had just checked in and put my stuff down. My poor boss. I was on the phone with him. He probably isn't going to hear right for a week. I screamed *loudly* when I saw her on the floor next to the bed."

I hadn't stopped to ask why Izzy had been there. I had assumed she had gotten involved because of her position at the local paper. *But why would a reporter be giving a statement to the police? Of course. She was a witness.* I shivered at the thought of being the one to discover a body. I still had nightmares about finding Jim on the beach.

Stacey inched forward on the bench. "What did she look like? Was she shot or something?"

Izzy tensed next to me.

I patted her arm and forced a smile onto my face. "So, what brings you two to town?"

"In honor of my late husband, Walter. He was the sweetest man. On our very first anniversary, he took me to a bed-and-breakfast out in Leavenworth. Unfortunately, it's closed down now." Stacey covered her mouth, her eyes misting, and slumped into the booth. "So instead, I try to find a new one every anniversary so I can still feel like we're together. May he rest in peace."

"I'm so sorry." I grabbed a tissue from my bag. "My condolences for your loss."

"And this whole business with that poor maid." Stacey grabbed the tissue and waved it. "It's… I don't even know what to say. It almost feels wrong celebrating my Walter's life at a time like this."

All of her motions were eye-catching and larger than life. She half covered her face as she dabbed at her eyes, peeking at me between each dab. I softened my expression to one of sympathy. She sniffled and clutched at the tissue.

Izzy cleared her throat and glanced over at Mason. "How about you?"

"I'm expanding my business. Luxury rental homes for retirees. There's a seasonal market out here for them."

"Were either of you there… when it happened?" I asked.

"Oh no," Stacey said. She leaned forward, placing her hands on the table.

I slid my hand under the table and touched it from underneath. It didn't always work, but I could sometimes pick up how people were feeling when we touched an object at the same time.

"I wanted to go exploring downtown, but it's so hard to do it alone. Luckily, Mason here volunteered to go with me. We were both getting ready when it happened. I had just finished putting on my lipstick when I heard the scream. And from what I heard from the sheriff, the poor girl had only been dead a few minutes when she was found. She was still warm. Can you imagine?" Stacey's eyes twinkled as she spoke.

The sensation I got through the table was one of curiosity. Stacey was being honest and, as her social media profile suggested, loved gossip a little too much. I didn't feel anything malicious or deceptive through the table. Neither of them would have seen anything, at least at the time of the murder. *Did they witness something important earlier?*

I cleared my throat. "Did either of you meet the maid?"

"I don't think so," Mason said. "It's possible she was the one changing out my sheets yesterday, but I was on a call, so I honestly can't say."

"I did." Stacey jumped back into the conversation. "She was such a sweet girl. She did her absolute best to accommodate the guests as much as possible. Even that peculiar one on the first floor."

"Oh?" I asked.

Stacey was practically on the edge of her seat, ready to continue. She didn't need any more prodding. She nodded, her eyes wide. "Oh yes. I tried to introduce myself to him at breakfast, but he had no interest in having any sort of conversation. Quite odd for the bed-and-breakfast crowd. Half of the appeal of these sorts of places is the people you meet. And he was so curt. Almost rude. He said he had to go to bed. To bed! Who sleeps after breakfast?"

"He got in late," Mason said.

"Not just in late. He went out late too." Stacey talked with her whole body, her hands swinging wide to emphasize words. "That fellow was in and out at all hours of the night. I could hear him slamming that front door at one in the morning."

I glanced at Izzy, but she was staring past me at the front door, a quizzical expression on her face. The door hadn't opened, and no one was there. I nudged her with my shoe, and she glanced between Stacey and me then back at the door again before dropping her head to study her hands. I chewed on my lip. Izzy was usually much more inquisitive. She must have been shaken up by finding the body.

"Did you see where he went off to? There isn't anything open that late around here," I said.

"If he does it again, I am this close"—Stacey held up her hand, her index finger and thumb almost touching—"to following him to see where he gets off to. But last night, I was much too tired to get out of bed. I had spent the day remembering Walter, after all. And well, his coming and going at odd hours isn't even the worst of it."

"Oh?" I asked another open-ended question.

It didn't matter what I said. Stacey was on a roll and wanted to share her hot gossip with whoever would listen. She nodded and leaned in closer, dropping her voice to a stage whisper. "I heard he declined to provide the sheriff with a statement."

My eyes widened. *Maybe this would be a quick investigation after all.* "Did he say why?"

"Too tired." Stacey crossed her arms. "Between you and me, I can't believe the sheriff let him get away with that. Even if he were sleeping, he could have done his civic duty and provided a statement."

Heather appeared at Stacey's side, holding two cups of coffee and a plate of scones. She handed a coffee each to Stacey and Mason and dropped the plate on the table between them.

Izzy leaned forward and stared past me at the door again. I caught her gaze and raised my eyebrow. She shook her head and sagged back into her seat. I glanced between her and the door. There was nothing there. *What does she keep looking at?*

Mason sipped his coffee, grabbed a scone, and rose to his feet. "I think I'm going to go take a walk."

Stacey scrambled after him. "I think that sounds wonderful. Mind if I join?"

Mason nodded. Before he could say another word, Stacey had looped her arm around his, and they sauntered out together as she loudly told him about a view she had been meaning to check out at the pier.

"How'd it go?" Heather slipped into the booth across from me.

"Okay. We got a potential lead. Stacey was a chatterbox." I

pulled out my phone. I had a message from Linda's best friend, Alyssa.

> **ALYSSA:**
> Thank you. I am about to break the news to the other girls. I'm sure they could use a plate of cookies after this.

"I got an in with Linda's friend," I said. "You got any spare cookies I can take to the sorority house?"

Heather nodded. "And if I don't, I can always bake some more."

"You're the best." I typed out a reply.

> **DANI:**
> I'll bring some by the house. Does today or tomorrow work best for you?

> **ALYSSA:**
> Tomorrow. 2 PM.

I shoved my phone into my pocket. "I've got a meeting with the best friend. You up for coming with me, Izzy?"

Izzy flinched and blinked. "Yeah. Just send me the details."

I peered into her face. "Are you okay?"

"I must be tired or something. I thought I heard someone saying my name." Izzy pinched the bridge of her nose. "What else do we have to do?"

I studied her for a second. *Not someone else acting out of character. I've got my hands full with Grace already.* My chest tightened, and a lump formed at the back of my throat. *I can't believe I just thought that. Jeez, Dani. Have a heart.* I forced myself to relax into my seat and smiled sympathetically at her. Finding a dead body would stress anyone out. "We have to interview the last guest."

"Right. Devin Clark? The guy on the first floor?" Izzy asked.

I checked my notes. We hadn't looked into him yet, so all I had was the name Heather had given me. I wrote a large question mark next to it. If Stacey was right, he was going to be a tough nut to crack.

"The meeting is tomorrow at two p.m. I'll text you the address."

Izzy nodded and hugged her arms to her body. She stared back at the front door and shivered. "Sounds like a plan."

"Are you feeling all right?" Heather asked.

Izzy yawned. "I'm just exhausted. I think I'm going to try to get some more sleep." She got up and shuffled to the door.

I tapped my fingers on the table as I went through the possibilities. The interview had some promise, but I'd learned nothing concrete. I had been hustled out of the crime scene so fast the day before that I didn't have time to look around in the hallway for clues. But I might have time today. Everyone at the bed-and-breakfast was either sleeping or out for a while.

"It looks like you have an idea percolating," Heather said.

"Do you think I could poke around on the second floor for a bit?"

She nodded. "I'll keep watch."

Heather put a note on the counter saying *Be back in 5,* then we went next door. She stood by the stairs as I walked down the hallway. I scanned the walls, looking for any art pieces with eyes. But I didn't find any. The flower theme continued throughout the hallway, but there weren't any bees in these pieces. It was all floral. I sighed. I had a spell that would let me look into the past through the memory of an object, but I could only see if the object had literal or metaphorical eyes. None of these did. "You really should consider having some animal art in the hallways."

Heather laughed. "Hindsight is twenty-twenty. I'll be putting up cameras in the hallways for safety later tonight."

The next-best option, if there wasn't an object to use, was

to purposefully activate my Sight with an obsidian mirror. Finding anything useful was a bit hit-or-miss. I could will it to focus on the murder, but it seemed to draw on the memories of people. I swallowed. *Will I see through the killer's eyes this time?*

I bounced in place, trying to loosen my tense muscles. The longer I put off casting the spell, the more uncertain I became about what I would see. Relaxing was a losing battle, so I gave up. I pulled out the obsidian mirror I kept in a side pocket of my purse and cast the spell to try to get a vision of the past.

Holding up the mirror, I looked into it with one eye and stared past it with the other so I could navigate better. But the mirror stayed dark. I moved it around and tried from a few different perspectives. It only showed something when I knelt on the ground. It was dim. *Am I seeing through Linda's eyes?* I lay on the floor and held the mirror above my head.

The image in the dark glass became clearer, though it was still murky, almost like I was seeing the world through slitted eyes. A pain shot through my back. It was a straight line, almost like I had banged against one of the steps. I could hear a man grunting, his phantom hands on my ankles. I tried to angle the mirror to see down my body, but the view became even more unfocused. Gritting my teeth, I shimmied down the carpet to get a better view. I probably looked ridiculous, flailing around on the ground on my back. I tried not to think about it as I focused on the mirror.

Something came into view. It was the only in-focus image I had seen. Green eyes stared down at me. They were wide, with dilated pupils. Then they disappeared. I dropped my arms down to my sides and released the spell.

"Did you find anything useful?" Heather asked.

I flipped onto my stomach and pushed myself up. "I could be wrong, but it sounded like a man. It was hard to tell. The only sound was grunting. Whoever it was pulled Linda down the hallway by her ankles. And they have green eyes."

"That should narrow it down."

"Hopefully." I put the mirror away and fixed my messy hair with my fingers. "It's not a common eye color. So in theory, only one of our suspects will have green eyes."

I followed her back down the stairs to the Bizzy Bean, where I gave her a quick hug goodbye. Heather promised to tell me the second she convinced Devin to speak with me. I texted Izzy the information for our meeting the next day and headed back to work. Two interviews down and two more to go. I hoped the next two would be as productive as the previous one. And fingers crossed, I would find the green-eyed man.

CHAPTER 5

The driveway was empty when I got home from work. My palms became sweaty on the steering wheel, and my stomach rolled. Grace wasn't home. I got out of the car and trudged up to the house, my feet heavy as I made my way up the porch steps and into the living room. Charlie greeted me at the door, his fluffy cat tail pointing straight up. I squatted to pick him up, grunting at the weight of him. He was just over six months old, and he was already pushing fifteen pounds. His paws were massive. I didn't know whether it was a side effect of his being a witch's familiar, or he was secretly the offspring of a very large breed.

"Has Grace been out long?" I asked him.

Charlie chirped. The emotions rolling off him were of loneliness and frustration. He had been alone for hours.

I scratched him under his chin as I retrieved a set of maps from under the coffee table. I flipped it open to the map of Point Pleasant and deposited Charlie next to it on the couch. "Okay, let's see where she parked her car."

The tracking spell came easily to me. That and heightening senses were two of my most practiced spells. I didn't need to read from the book anymore. Motes of light swirled out of my mouth and floated around me before settling onto the map. The lights gathered on the western side of town. My mouth went dry. Meredith's house was to the west. I leaned over the map and studied where the lights had congregated. They weren't over the house but a few blocks away at a trailhead. I exhaled and stepped back from the map. She could have easily walked back to Meredith's. Or she could be going on a hike, like she said she'd been doing.

I paced across the living room. Charlie hopped down from the couch and walked beside me. At each turn, he rubbed against my legs and purred.

"I told the Retirees I would let them know when she's out of the house." I fished my phone out of my pocket and dialed Betty's number.

"Is it time?" she asked when she picked up the phone.

I swallowed and fought the urge to simply nod. Spying on my daughter felt wrong. But not spying on her felt even worse. "Yes," I croaked.

I hung up and began pacing the room again. Charlie jumped onto a dining room chair and watched me as I walked back and forth. He was concerned and trying desperately to send me calming emotions.

I stopped at his chair and kissed him on the forehead. "I'm just worried about her, buddy."

He chirped at me as I turned away and continued with my pacing. After a few minutes, the pacing wasn't enough to keep my mind occupied. I moved on to cleaning. Mindless physical labor was calming. I washed the dishes by hand, swept the floors, and was halfway through mopping the kitchen floor when Betty's truck pulled up outside. I stowed the mop and bucket and met them at the front door.

The Retirees clustered together on the porch. They wore their usual matching tracksuits, that time in green. They shuffled inside as a group and stared at me. Agnes's shoulders were so tense that they were almost at her ears. Sarah hugged her arms to herself, her fingernails digging into the fabric of her jacket. And Betty's arms hung at her sides, her fingers tapping anxiously at her legs.

"Are you sure she's out?" Agnes asked.

I led them to the map and recast the tracking spell on Grace's car. It hadn't moved, still parked at the trailhead.

"We should be quick about this. It's a twenty-minute drive, and she could leave at any moment." Betty stared up the stairs, toward Grace's bedroom.

None of us moved. None of us felt good about snooping. Charlie rubbed against my leg, offering me strength.

I rolled my shoulders back to release the tension and strode up the stairs to her bedroom, the Retirees on my heels. We came to a stop outside her bedroom door, which was closed. The bedrooms didn't have locks, so getting inside wasn't a problem. It was getting in without her noticing that was going to be tough. Grace's psychometry abilities were stronger than mine. If we touched any of her things with our bare hands, she would be able to pick up our emotions. We wouldn't be able to hide our presence from her.

I held up a finger for them to wait then darted downstairs and out to my car. My claims adjuster kit was in my trunk. Over the years, I'd had to go out to some strange places and had collected an assortment of useful items, like plastic boot covers and gloves. I retrieved a pair of gloves for each of us and marched back upstairs to the waiting Retirees.

"Put these on."

"Good idea," Sarah said.

Once we all had our hands covered, I pushed open the bedroom door.

The curtains were drawn, leaving most of the room in deep shadow. Her bed was unmade. Clothes were piled around the dirty-clothes hamper instead of in it. My heart fluttered, but I pushed down the knot in my stomach and stepped inside.

My shoulders relaxed a little when nothing happened. I wasn't sure what I'd been expecting. A part of me had thought walking into the room would be like stepping into Meredith's house. But it wasn't. It was like any other room in my house.

Betty moved next to me. "I'll start with the dresser. Sarah, you take the closet. Agnes, the bed. And, Dani, could you search her nightstands?"

Betty always had a way of taking charge. I nodded and got to my assigned task. We moved around the room in silence as Charlie watched from the doorway. Betty started with the top drawer of the dresser and moved down. Sarah disappeared into the closet, her fingers searching through the few hanging garments in the back. I started with the nightstand closest to the door. She had a pair of headphones, a charger, a beaten-up novel, and random odds and ends that had been shoved into the first drawer. I ran my fingers underneath it to make sure there wasn't anything hidden below, but there was nothing.

I pulled open the drawer to the second nightstand. Inside were a half-empty bottle of melatonin and drawing pencils. I knelt next to the nightstand and shoved my hand underneath it.

"I found something," Agnes said.

She pulled a sketchbook from under the mattress. I climbed to my feet as the other Retirees converged on the bed. Agnes held the notebook out to me. My hands shook as I took it from her. *Calm down. It's just a—*

My thought died in my head as I flipped it open and was greeted with a realistic sketch of Meredith Walker, not as she had appeared as a spectral entity in the house when the group of us had ventured inside to figure out the origin of our family's curse but as she had appeared in my vision.

I slowly flipped from page to page. Each one contained realistic sketches of women. The first few were of Meredith, but then they shifted to sketches of Lillian Jones, Clara Price, and Edie Williams, my great-grandmother. Each drawing reminded me even more of the vision. Their hairstyles and clothing were the same. I stared at Lilian's face. Her jaw was set with determination. It was like it had been taken straight from my vision. It was the moment she stamped her foot and put up some sort of shield to protect the other women from Meredith's attacks.

I turned the notebook around and showed it to them. "This is my vision."

The Retirees exhaled as one and stepped even closer together.

"Does that mean she's had the same one? It could be her nightmare," I said.

"I don't know," Agnes replied.

"Divination isn't my strong suit." Sarah placed her hand on Agnes's shoulder. "But I know it's rare for two witches to have the same vision."

My stomach dropped. *If she didn't have the same vision, then how does she know what it looked like? Did she witness it some other way?* I swayed in place. This was all too much. I shoved the notebook back where Agnes had found it and fled the room.

The Retirees found me in the living room, curled up on the couch, with my knees pressed to my chest. Charlie wrapped himself around my head as Betty sat down on one side, and Agnes took the other. Sarah hovered in the middle of the room.

"This is new territory for us," Betty said.

"Then what am I supposed to do? This is too much." I stared ahead, wide-eyed, then I reached up and scratched Charlie behind his ears.

Agnes patted my back. "We need to pull in someone who specializes in mind magic."

"Isn't that what you specialize in?" I asked.

"There's more than one type. I specialize in illusions." Agnes sighed. "This is beyond that. It could be enchantment magic."

I dropped my feet to the floor and sat up. "Do you know someone who specializes in that?"

"We do." Betty's voice had a warning edge.

"Who?" I gripped Betty's hand.

"We can't tell you," Betty said.

"Why not?" I surged to my feet. "All these secrets. All they do is hurt people. Grace needs help now."

"We can't tell you." Sarah took a faltering step back.

Agnes stood and glared at the other Retirees. "But that doesn't mean we can't show her."

I glanced between the three of them. Betty sat glowering on the couch. Sarah didn't look any happier than Betty. And Agnes had a triumphant expression as they wilted in front of her.

"Fine." Betty stood and walked out the front door.

"Where are you going?" I darted after her.

"Just get in the truck," Betty grumbled as she climbed into the driver's seat.

Agnes marched to the truck. Sarah trailed behind her with her head hanging down. *They can't tell me, but they can show me? What on earth is going on?* I didn't think I would get an explanation. I glanced back at the living room. Charlie stared at me from the couch. *Sorry, buddy. I need you to stay here and keep an eye out for Grace.*

I followed the Retirees outside and climbed into Betty's truck. At the end of my driveway, we turned right, heading away from the heart of Point Pleasant and toward the outskirts of town.

I stared out the rear passenger window as the trees became thicker around the roadway. Betty turned onto a familiar route. There weren't many places to go along this road, and the farther she drove, the more apparent it became: we were going to Miller's Farm.

For months, I had been meeting Chris at the crossroads leading up to the farm for early-morning coffee dates. After he helped me with my first murder investigation, the sheriff had punished him by making him sit out there and monitor the nonexistent traffic early in the morning. I had never actually driven up to the farm. The Millers weren't well liked in town. There had never been a reason to go see any of them in person.

Agnes exhaled and covered her stomach with her hands. "We've got the threshold."

My eyes widened. Agnes's curse prevented her from leaving Point Pleasant without becoming ill. I studied her. The color leached from her face, and pinpricks of sweat formed along her brow.

"Are you going to be okay?" I put my hand on her shoulder.

Agnes nodded and shuddered. "So long as it's not a long visit. I'll just be a little queasy until we get back into town."

Betty turned in to the long driveway that led up to the farm. It wound through the trees. Almost all of them were the state's iconic evergreens. The pine trees loomed over the road, their needles littering the gravel. It was darker on the property, and there was a feeling of electricity in the air. I almost expected to shock myself when I shifted in my seat.

We drove out of the tree line. The farmhouse was three stories tall, with wooden shutters over every window. They reminded me of closed eyes. My heart skipped a beat when I saw the car parked outside the front door. It was Chris's SUV. *What's he doing here?*

The front door of the farmhouse opened, and Chris stepped onto the front porch with a woman trailing close behind. He towered over her in his deputy uniform. He'd gotten a haircut since I saw him last. His dark-brown hair was trimmed short over his ears. The woman next to him was solidly built, with strong forearms and chestnut-brown hair pulled back into a messy bun. She had a cunning glint in her eyes and a cruel edge to her smile as she stared up at Chris. The hairs on the back of my neck stood up. I didn't know what, but I knew with certainty she was going to do something to him.

With sweaty hands, I rolled down my window and cast the spell to heighten my senses. I knew it would be hard to hear what they were saying over the crunch of the gravel, but I had to try. I swayed in my seat as every sense peaked. The dim light was suddenly bright. My seat belt digging into my hip was agonizing. The scent of manure made me gag. And the sounds, they overwhelmed me. Birdsong mixed with the crunch of gravel and the roar of the truck's engine almost drowned out the sounds of their voices. I quickly shut down the senses I didn't need and focused in on what they were saying.

"I wish I had better news, Megan." Chris shoved a notepad into his pocket. "I appreciate how patient you're being while I try to figure out who keeps painting your cow."

"At least it was a different color this time." Megan barked a laugh. "You want me to top off your coffee before you head back into town?"

Chris nodded, and Megan stepped back into the house.

Betty parked the truck and gave me a dirty look. "Is that really necessary?"

I barely registered her words as Megan stepped back out onto her porch with a coffeepot in hand. Red petals swirled around the pot. Everyone's magic looked different, but this reminded me of a woman from the vision. *Ruby Miller. Miller's farm.* I didn't know how I had never made the connection before. But the Millers were witches. And Megan was about to use magic on my boyfriend—or who I hoped was still my boyfriend.

“Dani, wait!” Sarah grabbed my arm.

I slipped out of her grasp and launched myself out of the truck. I barreled up the driveway toward Chris as Megan refilled his thermos. Chris half turned toward me as I threw myself forward, knocking his thermos out of his hands.

“Dani, what—” Chris yelped as the hot coffee splashed down the front of him.

“I’m sorry. I can be such a klutz sometimes. Let me get that.” I knelt to pick up his thermos and fumbled with it, *accidentally* spilling the last of the coffee on the ground.

Chris grabbed it out of my hands. I blushed as he eyed the empty container.

Megan stared at me, hardness in her gaze, and smirked. “Oh my goodness. Let me go grab a towel.”

“No, it’s fine.” Chris shook his leg and glowered. “I really should be getting back.”

I stared after him as he strode toward his car. He probably thought I was nuts. But I couldn’t risk his drinking her enchanted coffee.

Sarah scrambled out of the truck and marched toward me as Betty helped Agnes out. Agnes looked even weaker. She swayed on her feet and gripped Betty’s arm as they plodded toward me. My gaze flicked between Chris’s car, Megan Miller, and the Retirees. This day was getting worse by the second.

I rounded on Megan. “What was in that coffee?”

“Dani, wait!” Sarah huffed as she came up next to me. She grabbed me by my shoulder and pulled me around. “Do you trust me?”

My eyes flicked between her and Megan. I did, but it felt wrong admitting it in front of this woman who had just tried to hurt someone I cared about.

“Do you trust me?” Sarah repeated.

I scowled and nodded.

“Okay. Then trust me for a little longer.” Sarah turned to

Megan. "Would you be a doll and go put on some more coffee?"

"Is this the Williams girl?" Megan asked.

"Yes, Dani is Mel's granddaughter."

Megan grunted and disappeared back inside.

I gaped at Sarah. *I trust her, but what is she thinking?* I lowered my voice to an angry whisper. "Do you have any idea where we are? Haven't you heard what the Millers are like? We can't trust this woman."

Agnes and Betty came to a stop next to me. They both glared at me, as if I were being the irrational one. *There's a reason no one in town trusts the Millers. And the Retirees just expect me to stand here and be nice?*

"Do you trust me?" Betty asked.

I sighed. "Of course I trust you."

Megan stepped back onto the porch with a cup of coffee. Red petals swirled around her hands. Up close, they were translucent, more like red lights that were petal shaped. She raised her eyebrow and held out the cup of coffee.

"If you trust me, if you want to protect your daughter, then you will drink that." Betty crossed her arms.

I blanched at the idea. I looked from Retiree to Retiree. All three of them stared back at me with the same expression, exasperation mixed with a little bit of amusement. *They think this is funny?* I stared at the offered mug. *They expect me to drink that potion?* When their facial expressions didn't change, I reached for the mug. It was plastic, so it wouldn't break. I eyed it suspiciously and sniffed. It smelled like coffee.

Grumbling, I clutched the protective amulet I wore and drank.

My eyes widened. It was like a curtain had lifted. The smirk on Megan's face shifted to a sad smile. The cruelty in her eyes faded into apprehension. She hugged her arms to her body as if ready to bolt at any second. The woman I had been so sure was up to no good a moment before was suddenly a regular woman.

I spun in place and looked at the farm. The deep shadows were no longer as dark. The shutters over the windows were just shutters. In an instant, the farm shifted from a place that felt foreboding to a cozy home.

"What just happened?" I asked.

Sarah sighed. "We can't tell you."

"Why not?" I demanded.

"It's complicated." Sarah wrung her hands. "We technically can, but then, we would be breaking a promise to a Miller. And breaking a promise to a Miller comes with a nasty backlash."

Megan sighed. "If I knew how to get you out of the promise, you know I would."

What on earth is going on? I glanced between the women.

Megan hung her head. "Do you know who Ruby Miller was?"

I nodded. "A member of my great-grandmother Edie's coven."

"The original cursed coven." Megan shifted uncomfortably. "And we all have different curses, right?"

I nodded again. "My Sight activates whenever it pleases."

"And my family is distrusted by everyone. It's instinctual. You don't even have to meet us. Just hear our names, and you automatically distrust us. It makes things difficult." Megan took the mug back from me. "My great-grandmother was nervous that one of you guys, the other descendants, would fall victim to that distrust and tell nonwitches about us."

"It wasn't an unfounded fear," Betty said.

"After the curse, the coven fractured," Sarah added.

"So my great-grandmother made everyone promise they would tell no one that the Millers were witches and made it a binding spell." Megan rolled her eyes. "But it was a promise to her. And I can't figure out how to end a promise when the person it was made to isn't around to release it anymore. Now, it causes more harm than good. It's a pain to deal with."

"And the spelled coffee? What does it do?" I asked.

"It helps you see clearly. At least when it comes to me and my family. There are some broad protections against mind-altering effects, but they usually just tone things down a notch. Like lowering the volume. The effects are still there. It's just weakened. If you want to nullify it completely, you have to have a targeted defense. The coffee does that. I'll share the spell with you."

"Hasn't it already been fixed?" I asked.

"For now." Megan sighed. "But it always comes back. Even the best defense needs maintenance. Usually only once a month, though. Something about the full moon messes with it."

"And because the coffee has to do with your curse, they couldn't tell me about it?"

Megan nodded.

Agnes swayed on her feet.

Megan darted forward to grab her other arm. "I'm surprised you're out here. It must be serious."

"It is," Betty said.

"Let me get you inside so you can at least sit down while we talk." Megan led the way into her home.

The space was filled with hand-carved antique furniture. It was well maintained and obviously loved. The scent of roasting apples filled the air. A cool breeze cut through the living room from an open window in the kitchen that looked over the backyard. I paused in the doorway and stared. The largest cow head I had ever seen, painted bright purple, was thrust through the open window. Its tongue was sticking out as it tried to sneak an apple off the counter.

"Gertie!" Megan walked over and grabbed the apple from the counter. "We talked about this. No licking the counter. If you want an apple, ask for one."

The cow snorted and held open its mouth.

I stared wide-eyed as Megan hand fed the cow a few apples. Once it had claimed its third one, she turned back to us. Agnes had made her way to a chair at the dining room table, with Betty at her side. Sarah hovered over them. I shook my head. Instead of being a bad day, it was now a strange day. I took a seat next to Betty and waited for Megan to sit down.

"So..." Megan cleared her throat. "What brings you to my neck of the woods?"

"It's our turn to ask if you've heard of a name," Agnes said. She was getting paler by the minute. Her hands shook as she pushed her damp hair away from her face. "Have you ever heard of Meredith Walker?"

Megan pursed her lips and slouched, crossing her arms. "The name sounds familiar."

"She's the one who cursed our families. And we found where she did it too. We found her house," Sarah said, continuing where Agnes had left off.

Megan smiled. "That's great."

Betty shook her head.

"How is it not?" Megan straightened in her seat.

"Because there's something wrong with the house," I said.

"It's a place where a curse happened." Megan stood. There was a bounce in her step as she walked back into the kitchen to put the kettle on. "It would surprise me if there was nothing wrong with it at all."

"And it's been magically guarded by a group of Wardens of the West," Betty said.

Megan tensed and turned slowly toward us. "Are they here?"

"No," I said. "But... the wrongness of the house has infected my daughter."

Megan whistled and leaned back against the counter. "Infected how?"

I shifted in my seat. Being a witch was still so new to me. It felt strange to explain things, especially since I was the least knowledgeable person in the room. So I told her everything, about our discovery of the house, our first foray inside, where Grace had gotten a splinter before we saw the warning sigils. I told her about my vision, and I finished by telling her how the appearance of Grace's magic had slowly shifted to look more and more like Meredith Walker's. By the time I was done, she was sitting on the floor of her kitchen, her legs sprawled out in front of her, her mouth hanging open.

"Wow, that's... a lot." Megan pushed herself back up to standing and walked over to the table on shaky legs. She plopped down in a chair and stared at her hands. "You're here because you're worried its mind control."

Agnes nodded. "And you're the only one who really understands that type of magic."

Megan gave a hard, sarcastic laugh. "Enchantments and mind control are two different things."

"They're related." Sarah sniffed.

"True." Megan sighed. "But from what you've just told me, mind control is the better of the two options."

"What?" My heart skipped a beat. *How could mind control be a better option? Better than what?*

Megan grimaced. "This could also be a possession."

The Retirees shifted closer together. Whenever they heard bad news, they leaned on one another for support.

"Like a demon?" I asked.

Megan shrugged. "More like a ghost. But they're dangerous. And the only way to deal with a possession is with a necromancer. And we are fresh out of those."

It felt like the world had dropped out from underneath me. A good-case scenario was that my daughter was being mind controlled. And a worst-case scenario was that she was being possessed by a ghost—one none of us could do anything about.

"I know a smidge. Enough to do a séance if needed. Identify the presence of a ghost. But a possession is outside my wheelhouse."

My mind floundered, and I latched on to the only sentence that gave me hope. She could identify the presence of one. "Does that mean you could tell me if she's possessed?"

"I could. I would just need to talk to her. Or if you can't bring her here, if I had a sample of her, I could perform some magic on it to figure it out."

I furrowed my brow. "A sample of her?"

"Like a strand of her hair. Something from near the head or heart works best. All magic leaves a residue. A possession is a type of magic, just not a type we can do. But I can read the residue and determine if it's mind control or possession. And if I can't, it's some unknown third option."

"Okay." I swallowed and rubbed my sweaty palms on my jeans. "I can do that. I can get some of her hair for you."

"Once you have it, bring it to me, and I'll get to work. It can take a few days for me to figure it out sometimes."

Agnes swayed and slumped forward. She rested her head on the wood table, her breathing labored. I scrambled to my feet and crouched next to her, peering into her face. Her eyes were squeezed closed, but she was still conscious.

"We need to leave," Betty said.

Sarah wrapped her arm around Agnes's shoulders, and Betty took the other side. They hoisted Agnes to her feet and shuffled together to the front door. Megan stood and grabbed Betty's purse, which she had dropped in her haste to get out. She held it out to me.

"Thank you for your help." I took the purse from her.

"If it weren't for Lori's clear-sight potion, I wouldn't have any friends. It's only fair that I return the favor."

I swallowed. My mother's name didn't come up in

conversation much. She was an absentee mother who I hadn't seen since my daughter was born. It felt strange hearing Megan say something nice about her. The only thing that I could rely on when it came to Lori was that I couldn't count on her. She always left when I needed her most. I walked to the door in a daze.

Megan followed me and stared after us until we had loaded Agnes into the truck. She was still standing in the doorway when we entered the tree line, and she disappeared from view.

My heart quivered as we drove down the long, winding driveway. I stared at Agnes. She sat with her head leaning against the window, her eyes fluttering open and closed. She had pushed herself too hard trying to support me. Her curse really was a prison. But in a way, all of ours were. Agnes's was just a bit more literal.

I couldn't imagine how lonely it must be to have a curse like Megan's. Guilt washed over me as I replayed the encounter in my head. I had accused her of trying to hurt Chris, when all she had been doing was ensuring he continued to see her as she was. *A person who likes my mother. Is there something—*

I cut the thought off before it got too far. My mother had abandoned me, and that was all I needed to know. There was no coming back from that. *Or is there? Why does everything keep getting more complicated? Maybe having a murder investigation to keep me distracted isn't such a bad idea after all.*

CHAPTER 6

The morning at work had been productive. I had completed two home inspections, one for water damage from a suspected burst frozen pipe and the second for a small kitchen fire. It was helpful to have something active to keep my mind distracted. If I let myself sit and think too long, my mental wheels would start spinning again. But it was unproductive spinning, like I was stuck on a hamster wheel. My thoughts bounced from the case to my daughter to Chris to Charlie, who was annoyed with me at home, and back to the case with no clear dots connecting the thoughts. I had been glad for the change of pace. When I ran out of things to do at work, I walked across the hall to see Olivia.

Bailey, Olivia's new puppy, greeted me at the door, her long tongue lolling out of her mouth. She had a goofy grin on her wide face as she pranced around me, her golden coat shimmering under the office lights. When I knelt to pet her, she immediately flopped onto her back for belly rubs. "You are going to put Charlie out of a job if you keep up these friendly greetings."

Olivia poked her head out of the break room in the back. She had her hair up in a double puff with a red headband positioned in front. The headband perfectly matched her red sweater dress. She smiled when she saw me. "I was just about to sit down for lunch. Do you want to join me?"

My stomach grumbled at the mention of food. Stress made me forget to eat, which was sometimes dangerous—especially with how much energy casting spells took out of me. I nodded and ran back to my office to get my lunch box.

I hadn't sat in the break room of the Pleasant View Insurance Agency since I had helped organize the office after my grandmother's death. We shared a foyer and visited often, but I hadn't had a reason to be back in the employee area since I sold the book of business to Olivia. It felt nostalgic to be back there and calmed my nerves. I sank into the chair and took my time eating my canned soup.

"I'm glad you popped by. I was hoping to chat with you about something," Olivia said.

I paused, my spoon halfway to my mouth. "Oh?"

"Are you still interested in working with my dad on his downtown revitalization project?"

Her father, Steven Bishop, was the newly elected mayor. He had made it his personal mission to make Point Pleasant thrive.

"Maybe?" I had suggested that the next project be repairing the historic sheriff's station downtown, which had been badly damaged in a water leak a few years back, and ever since, the sheriff had been operating out of a couple of run-down double-wides at the edge of town. Then I'd been quickly cajoled into volunteering. I had, of course, made the suggestion before Chris asked for space. Now, it was just awkward. "When would it start?"

"They approved it this morning. They're drawing up paperwork and are hoping to start taking bids from contractors in two weeks."

I dropped my spoon into my bowl. I didn't know how messy my life would be in two weeks. Everything could be better, or if my luck held, it could be infinitely worse. "I'm not sure…"

"We really could use help vetting them. My dad doesn't have any construction experience, and the council members are a librarian, a restaurant owner, and a lawyer. They don't have much experience in that either."

I sighed. I couldn't bear the thought of letting Olivia down. She had been a rock for me when my gran passed. "Okay. I'll do it."

She squealed with excitement. "Thank you! Thank you! I'll let him know."

We spent the rest of lunch chatting about strange claims, a storm that was brewing over Canada that was projected to come south later that week, and the joys of parenthood. Her baby, Xander, was growing faster than she could keep up. For the first time that day, time slid past quickly. Before I knew it, it was almost twelve thirty, and I had to run if I wanted to make my meeting with Alyssa in Seattle by two.

I rechecked the gift basket Heather had put together before driving off the ferry in Mukilteo. It was loaded with six different types of cookies, two different hot cocoa mixes, a slew of mini marshmallows, and some tension-tamer tea. She was well practiced at building these kits. Everything sat perfectly inside the basket. My mouth watered as I looked at the cookies.

The drive down to the University of Washington was smoother than usual. There weren't many cars on the road that time of day, so I made it down there in less than forty minutes. I found a place to park in one of the parking garages and carried the overflowing basket a few blocks to the sorority house, a redbrick building with a well-manicured lawn out front. Large shrubberies clustered around the building.

I paused before crossing the street and pulled out my phone. I had expected Izzy to meet me, but she wasn't anywhere in sight.

> **DANI:**
> Are you still on your way?

> **IZZY:**
> I am so sorry. I fell asleep. I'm not used to sleeping in strange places, and I was up half the night. Old buildings make strange noises.

> **DANI:**
> I'm already here. Any questions you wanted answered in particular?

> **IZZY:**
> My brain is still mush. You ask great questions, though. I'm sure you'll ask everything I would have thought of.

> I am really looking forward to the construction being done at my apartment. Stupid water leak from the unit above has me all discombobulated. Maybe I should have just gone to a hotel. I thought a bed-and-breakfast would be cozy and fun.

> **DANI:**
> It usually is. Once this is all over, you should try it again. I'll update you when I'm done.

> **IZZY:**
> Thank you!

I shoved my phone into my pocket and strode across the street. In the few times I had worked with Izzy, she had been a lot more reliable. I chewed on my lip as I walked, vacillating between annoyance and worry. Discovering the body seemed to weigh on her more than I would have expected. *Should I talk to her about it?* I hadn't decided by the time I reached the front door of the sorority house. I pushed that train of thought to the back of my mind and knocked.

I studied the owl engraving above the door until Alyssa Warren pulled it open. Her shoulder-length warm-brown hair hung loose around her face. She was still dressed in her pajamas, an oversize T-shirt featuring a band I didn't recognize over flannel pants. Her eyes were red rimmed.

"You must be Dani." Alyssa sniffed. "It's so thoughtful of you to drive all the way down here. Please, come in."

I followed Alyssa inside. It was a beautiful building. The wooden floors flowed from the front door, throughout the open foyer and living room, and down a hallway into other areas of the house. We passed girls in clusters of four to five, sitting in various meeting rooms, as we made our way through the house to the kitchen. There was a heaviness in the air. All of them had the same red-rimmed eyes as Alyssa. The news of Linda's death had spread. It must have been shocking to lose a housemate to violence.

As we passed through the hallways, I mumbled the words to the relaxation spell over the bundle of cookies. I wasn't sure which one she would want to eat, so I hit them all with my magic, turning each cookie into a mini relaxation potion. They helped put whoever ate them into a calmer state, and it was easier to trust people when you were calm—which was very helpful during interviews. The small golden lights of my magic sank into the food until the entire bundle glowed in my arms.

We came to a stop in the kitchen, which was almost twice the size of Heather's kitchen. A series of six fridges took up one wall, and there were three commercial-size ovens. Clipboards were posted by the far door, where the girls checked off their house-cleaning duties. It looked like whoever was in charge of organizing the house ran a tight ship.

I put the basket on the counter and turned it around so Alyssa would see all the cookie options. "The peanut butter chocolate chip are my favorite, but they're all good."

Alyssa studied the cookies for a few seconds before selecting a lemon crinkle cookie. She took a tentative bite. The soft glow of the cookie flowed into her and settled in her skin.

I gave her a sympathetic smile. "I just wanted to say I am so sorry for your loss. Linda was such a sweet girl. The bed-and-breakfast won't be the same without her."

"Thank you," Alyssa mumbled around her cookie. "The girls are taking it hard. I've been doing my best to keep it all together."

I rested my hip against the counter. "It was just so shocking, you know?"

Alyssa shrugged. "I wish I were shocked, but I've been worried something might happen to her for weeks now."

Surprised, I asked, "Why?"

"Her boyfriend is a real piece of work." Alyssa grabbed a second cookie. It snapped in her fingers. "I wish I could be there when they take him in."

"What makes you so sure he did it?"

"I've had a bad feeling about that guy since they first met six months ago. What thirty-four-year-old still hangs out at college bars? He gave me the creeps. And after they began dating, he got really controlling. It started with what she wore, then he moved on to who she could hang out with. I don't know if you've ever been part of Greek life, but... interacting with the fraternities is just something you do. We have joint events. Fundraisers. The whole nine. And he convinced her to back out of every event that had her working with men. It was ridiculous." She moved her hands wildly as she spoke, not noticing the crumbs from the broken cookie falling to the floor.

"Wow." I left it open-ended. It was clear she had a lot on

her mind, and letting people in her position vent was usually more productive than trying to guide the conversation, at least at the beginning.

Alyssa shoved half the cookie into her mouth and chewed on it. The relaxing effect of the spell was at war with her anger, the lights of the spell flickering under her skin. "He was trying to get her to leave the sorority and move in with him off campus. And I could tell where that was going. The second she moved in, he would have cut her off from her other friends. She would have been completely isolated. It's how those things go."

"Did you ever see him hurt her?"

Alyssa shook her head. "I didn't have to. We've all seen those Reddit stories. Young women getting involved with a narcissist. He had all the red flags."

It was like the wind went out of her sails. She slumped forward, her shoulders rounded inward, and hugged her arms to her body. Tears welled in her eyes. "I should have been there with her. I knew she was planning on telling him she wasn't moving in with him. I knew it, but I didn't go. I wanted her to want me there. I wanted her to ask. But I should have offered."

I put a hand on her shoulder. "There's no way you could have known."

She wiped at her eyes. "I thought he was a bad dude. And she was my best friend in the whole world. Why didn't I just offer?"

I rubbed her back while she cried. The lights from the spell I had cast were going out one by one in the bags of cookies. I swallowed. I didn't want to push her, but I didn't have much longer until the little calm my magic had provided her would be gone. The glow in her skin was fading. It was barely visible under the fluorescent lights of the kitchen.

"Have you seen him since it happened?" I asked.

"No." She straightened and wiped at her eyes. "But I know where he's going to be. If he isn't back at that bar where he and Linda met tomorrow, I'll be surprised. He doesn't strike me as someone who's okay with his bed being empty for long. And Friday nights are always busy."

The dim light of the spell went out, and she curled into herself again and sobbed. "I should have been there."

I patted her shoulder again, but she barely registered my presence. I expressed my condolences again and backed out of the kitchen. The sounds of girls crying followed me to the front door. Closing it behind me, I shut my eyes. There was a stark contrast between inside the house and outside it. The sounds of laughter from students strolling down the street mixed with birdsong and the steady hum of traffic.

I shook myself and walked back to my car, where I pulled up Linda's profile on my phone. The number of farewell posts on her wall had tripled since I last checked it. First, I checked her relationship status. No one was linked there. *Hiding the boyfriend from the parents? Or is he just not on social media much?* I scrolled through her feed, going further back than I had before. Alyssa was right. Her fashion had become more conservative over the past six months, and the number of posts she had where she tagged men and women had gone down. In all of her recent activity, it was just girls from her sorority or family. I pursed my lips and continued searching until I found a selfie of Linda standing outside a bar. Her hazel eyes were bright and filled with joy. She had a secretive smile on her face. The tag read *"Just had the best date night ever."* In the background, I could make out the name of the bar: the Thirsty Dragon.

Grinning, I texted Izzy. I might not have a name yet, but I had a location. And a guy supposedly grieving a dead girlfriend would stand out. If it was one he frequented, the bartender would probably know who he was.

DANI:
I got a lead. I'll give you a full download tomorrow.

IZZY:
Excellent. I just bumped into Devin, the mystery guest from the first floor. Wish me luck. I'm going to try to convince him to come have coffee with us in the morning.

My smile widened further. It had been a very productive day after all.

CHAPTER 7

I arrived just after nine in the morning at the Bizzy Bean. Because I had been there so often over the past few days, it was beginning to feel like a second home to me. Since my last visit, the local artist who painted the front window had come by and put up a new display. They had become very skilled at melding the bee theme with the cats that now lived inside. Featured on the main window were the latest batch of kittens Heather was fostering, with the mighty Muffin taking center stage. She had been painted standing on her rear legs, her little paws overhead as she tried to catch a bee flying through the group. I could tell it was Muffin because she had very distinctive markings on her cheek fluff that made her look like she had the most exaggerated cat eye in history.

"It turned out really cute, didn't it?" a man next to me asked.

I jumped at the sound of his voice. It was the same guy from the day before. He had an earnest expression as he held out a clipboard toward me.

"Do you know much about orcas?"

I shook my head and stepped away. "Sorry. I've got some-place to be."

Becca was behind the counter when I entered the café. I waved as I made my way into the plexiglass enclosure to find Izzy. The second I was through the door, the kittens swarmed me. They swatted playfully at my laces as I crossed the room, forcing me to carefully pick up my feet as I walked.

Izzy was sitting at a round table in the middle of the room. My eyes flicked to the booth in the back. It was empty, and I was half tempted to ask her to move. But I didn't need to sit in my usual spot. I just liked it. Sighing, I took a seat opposite her at the table.

Izzy smiled weakly. She wore a cute black woolen wrap dress with expertly applied makeup that almost hid how exhausted she was.

"You doing okay?" I asked.

She shrugged. "I'm a really light sleeper."

"When are you getting back into your apartment?"

"Three or four days? It depends on how long it takes for the place to dry out. I'll still be missing part of my ceiling, but that's better than being in a strange bed." Izzy yawned. "Good news, though—Devin's going to be down in a few minutes for drinks."

We didn't have long to chat before he arrived, so I quickly told her about my interview with Alyssa. "I was planning on trying to track down the boyfriend tonight."

"That's a great idea." Izzy's eyes flicked to the door behind me, and her smile widened as she stood, waving someone over. "Devin, over here."

I turned and watched him approach. He was slim. His shaggy brown hair, which did nothing to soften his sharp features, fell into his green eyes.

I stiffened. The killer had green eyes. I studied him, trying to get a feel for who he was, before he sat down. He wore black jeans and a ratty green hoodie with the sleeves pulled down to cover his palms. I had never seen someone who looked so uncomfortable in his own skin. He walked with his shoulders rolled forward, his gaze furtively darting back and forth around the room. His pace slowed as he noticed me, and he smiled awkwardly as he took a chair between us.

"Devin, this is my friend Dani. Dani, this is Devin. I hope you don't mind that my friend is here."

"Not at all." Devin drummed his fingers on the edge of the table.

I placed my hand on the wood. Devin had been the last one to touch it, so I could pick up traces of how he was feeling through touch. My skin tingled, and my heartbeat sped up. *Surprise? Poor guy probably thought this was a date.*

"Are you staying at the bed-and-breakfast too?" I asked.

Devin nodded. "Been there for a few days. I like staying downtown."

"Point Pleasant has such a charming downtown," Izzy said. "Have you been here before?"

Devin shook his head and drummed his fingers on the table again. "First time on Whidbey Island."

"What brings you here?" I asked.

He narrowed his eyes. "Just traveling."

Through the table, the sensation shifted. My muscles tensed, and my stomach tightened. I forced myself to relax into my seat. People had a tendency to subconsciously mimic the people around them. When you were talking to someone completely calm, it was hard to stay anxious for too long. The urge, at least for most people, was to meet them where they were emotionally.

"That's exciting," Izzy said. She leaned forward, placing her hands on the table. "I wish I got to travel more."

My throat closed as the frustration from Izzy warred with the wariness from Devin. Their emotions blended together. I pulled my hand back from the table. A cold read would not be helpful.

"You want a coffee?" I asked. Maybe a calming spell would help.

"No, thanks." Devin said.

I slumped in my seat.

"So, how long are you going to be in town?" Izzy asked.

"I'm not on a specific schedule." Devin shrugged.

Talking to that guy was like pulling teeth. I studied him. He alternated drumming his fingers on the edge of the table with picking at his cuticles. He was a ball of anxious energy, ready to bolt at any second. I had to get the focus of the conversation on Linda sooner rather than later and hope that something useful came of it. I forced a smile onto my face. "So, how are you enjoying staying at the bed-and-breakfast? Isn't the bee theme just adorable?"

His eyes flicked toward me then the door. He shrugged again. "It's been okay."

"It really is too bad about that girl who died." Izzy shuddered.

Devin chewed on his fingernails, his leg bouncing under the table. "Yeah."

"She was a sweet girl. Did you have the opportunity to meet her?" I asked.

His mouth quirked at the corner. "She served breakfast two days ago."

I fought the urge to groan. Interviewing him was almost impossible. He answered the questions exactly, no more, no less. Most people liked to elaborate.

"You sure you don't want a coffee?" I asked.

Devin shook his head. "Izzy, did you want one? My treat."

"Sure." Izzy smiled.

Devin stood and scurried out of the plexiglass enclosure.

I scooted forward and lowered my voice. "I'm not sure if we're going to get anything together on this one. It looks like he was here to see you and not to see your older friend. I'm feeling a little like a third wheel."

Izzy winced. "You're probably right. Divide and conquer, then?"

I nodded. "I'll take the boyfriend, and you take Devin?"

Izzy shivered and hugged her arms to her body, despite it being warm inside the café. "Sounds good."

"Are you feeling all right?"

"There was a sudden breeze."

I raised my eyebrow but let it go. If she wanted to work through a cold, that was her decision. I would just have to make sure I was taking some vitamin C supplements so I didn't catch whatever flu she was fighting off.

Devin arrived back at the table and set a cup of coffee down in front of Izzy.

I stood as he took his seat. "It was great meeting you, Devin, but I've gotta head out."

He visibly relaxed and smiled. It was a nice smile that made his sharp features a little less intense. "It was nice meeting you too."

As I crossed the Bizzy Bean, my mind was already on the next step in the investigation. Alyssa hadn't given me much information about Linda's mysterious boyfriend. I shuddered as I stepped out onto the street and a cool breeze hit me. I zipped my coat up and hunched my shoulders as I marched to my car. When I reached it, I faltered at the door. She hadn't given me a name. I had no way of digging into who this guy was. *Heather might know.*

DANI:
Did Linda ever talk to you about her boyfriend?

HEATHER:
She mentioned him in passing a few times.

DANI:
What was his name?

HEATHER:
I think he called in for her once. I might still have it written down somewhere. Let me check.

I shoved my phone into my pocket and slid into the front seat of my car. Sighing, I started the engine. On days like that, it felt like I lived in my car. I had at least three home inspections I had to get done before the day's end, so I would spend more time in my car than out of it. My first was in Gig Harbor, which would take me well over two hours to get to. Traffic around Seattle that time of day was going to be a beast. Then I had to drive up to Everett. I would be criss-crossing Seattle all day. It made me groan to think about ending my day there, and I hoped my interview with the boyfriend was worth all the time in the car.

CHAPTER 8

Traffic heading into Seattle from my last inspection in Marysville was worse than I'd thought it would be. It crawled forward, car length by car length, for over an hour before the pace finally picked up. To pass the time, I alternated between making work calls to update insurance companies on the status of my claims investigations and snacking on the miscellaneous items I had in my purse. I had stupidly skipped dinner, and I needed to make sure my energy reserves were up in case I needed to cast any spells during the interview. Two Snickers, a power bar, and a package of trail mix later, my mouth was dry, but I was mostly full.

I found a spot to park in an overpriced parking garage a few blocks from the Thirsty Dragon and checked my phone. Heather had responded while I was driving. She didn't have a last name, but his first name was Josh. I quickly checked Linda's social media again. There were two Joshes, but neither one looked right. One of them was a twelve-year-old cousin, and the other was over sixty. Grumbling, I put my phone back into my pocket and trudged the three blocks to the bar.

The outside of the bar was relatively nondescript. It had

the same brick construction as a lot of the buildings in the UW district. I pushed the door open and stopped. Inside was an entirely different story. It had a medieval theme. The waitresses wore corseted barmaid dresses with flowing white shifts underneath and had their hair up in braided circlets around their heads. Peanut shells covered the floor, and music that reminded me of a Ren faire blasted through the speakers. It was loud and very crowded.

I pushed through the mass of people, my eyes swiveling from side to side as I made my way to the bar. Almost everyone had a drink in their hand, and the oldest person there was maybe twenty-six. I came to a stop at the bar. The medieval theme continued to the menu, which was filled with ales, wines with Elven-sounding names, and a wide variety of mixed drinks with interesting names like *the Noble Pursuit.* The bartender wore a leather apron over a white tunic and had an impressive handlebar mustache that took up a large part of his face.

"What can I get you?" he asked.

"Just a Coke," I said.

He grunted and grabbed a tankard from the stack behind him. "You a DD?"

"You could say that." I leaned over the bar. "My daughter's friend asked me to come keep an eye on Josh, given what happened. You seen him yet?"

He nodded. My gamble had paid off. Alyssa had said he was a regular, so it made sense that the bartender would know him. He cocked his head to the side. "End of the bar in his usual spot."

I smiled and backed away with my tankard in hand.

The bar was massive. It cut across the back of the room and curved at the end to continue into a billiards room at the back. Josh sat at the end of the bar, just past the curve. From his vantage point, he could see the entrance, down both sides of the bar, and the doors to the bathrooms.

I melted back into the crowd and studied Josh from a spot near the front door. If I didn't know he was in his thirties, I wouldn't have guessed it. He was a tall man, easily over six feet, and had broad shoulders. His dirty-blond hair was cut short on the sides, but the top was longer. As I watched him, he finished his beer and slid it across the counter before ordering the next one. He had something predatory about him. His body language said brooding, but the way his eyes moved over the crowd was more man-on-the-prowl. A lot of women fell for the brooding-artist routine, especially when they were younger, which gave me the impression that the expression was for show. It didn't match up with his eyes at all. I couldn't make out what color they were, but they were a lighter color.

Is that his second beer? Or has he had more drinks than that? I mentally went through the possibilities. I had never used the relaxation-potion spell on a drunk person before and wasn't sure how it would interact with alcohol. And something about how his eyes lingered on certain women made me think he wouldn't stop to talk to me. If they looked older than twenty-two, his eyes just slid past them, almost like they weren't there at all. *Would he even talk to an older woman?*

I smiled. Luckily for me, I didn't have to look like me in order to interview him. I made my way to the bathroom and ducked into an empty stall as the bathroom door opened up behind me. Heels scraped against the tile floor as the woman swayed outside the stall door. I rolled my shoulders back and closed my eyes. Normally, I had a mirror I could watch myself in to make sure it worked. Casting the spell over a toilet was awkward. The motes of light swirled around me and settled into my skin. It was warm. I held the idea of a woman in my head. I imagined young, pretty, and blond. It was easiest to keep it simple. I had to hold that idea in my head the entire time I maintained the illusion, or it would slip. I really wished I knew how to tie a spell off like

Kimberlee Jones had showed me so I could maintain it without thinking about it. Someday, I would learn that trick —if I could ever convince her to tell me why she didn't like me.

I pulled out my phone and studied my reflection on the black screen. The glamor spell had worked. I looked like a twenty-year-old college student with brown eyes instead of my usual gray.

I pushed the stall door open. The woman standing in the bathroom wore a tiny red dress. She cocked her head to the side and opened her mouth. She closed it, shook her head, and toddled past me.

A second after I exited the bathroom, I felt eyes on me. I glanced at the bar. Josh had noticed me. He held my gaze for a second before looking away then glanced back and held my eyes again. I smiled, and as I crossed the room, I snapped a photo of him on my phone in case I needed to track him down later. Then I hopped onto a stool next to him.

"I don't think I've seen you in here before," he said. His eyes were green, just like the killer's. There wasn't any sadness in his expression. Instead, there was hunger.

"Oh." I swallowed, my mind floundering. I should have given more thought to my cover story. He was alone. Alyssa was right. He didn't seem like someone who wanted to have his bed empty that night, which made him seem unsentimental. I had to make him think being sad would appeal to me somehow. I found myself faking a Valley girl accent. "The name looked interesting. I don't actually go here. My sister lost a housemate this week, so I'm visiting to help cheer her up."

"A housemate?"

I nodded. "Yeah. A girl died or something. I think my sister said she was murdered."

He stiffened at *murdered*. "A Theta girl?"

I nodded again. "It was so hard to stay in there. I've never been sure what to do around people who are grieving. I just want to do whatever I can to help, and when no one knows what they need, I flounder. And no one knows what they need when they're sad like that. You know what I mean?"

"I get that." He shifted closer to me on his stool and lowered his gaze. When he raised his eyes back up to meet mine, they were filled with intensity. It didn't quite look like sadness. But it could pass for it if I weren't scrutinizing his every movement. "It's been so hard. I haven't been able to bring myself to go into that house since it happened."

"You knew Linda?" I asked, feigning shock.

He lowered his gaze again and wiped at an invisible tear. "She was my girl for a while."

"I am so sorry."

He reached out and touched my arm. "I'm trying to live in the moment. A distraction would be wonderful."

My skin crawled at the feel of his hand. It took everything I had to hold the mental image of the illusion and to smile sadly at the same time. I swallowed and forced myself to stay still. *Maybe I should have questioned him looking like me. All this guy seems to want is to get laid. What a creep.* I focused on the mental image and plowed forward with the next question. "You must be Josh. I heard she was planning on moving in with you or something."

He pulled his hand back and took another drink of his beer. "Honestly, I'm not sure if I wanted her after the way she had been behaving lately."

I blinked. "What do you mean by that?"

His shoulders tensed, and his voice came out bitter. "I want my girl to put me first. The past few weeks, all she could do was talk about her uncle."

"Oh?" I left the question open-ended. He was mad about something, and I wanted to give him the opportunity to get it off his chest.

"He disappeared from her life when she was a kid then

showed back up out of the blue. And she was obsessed with him. Brian this and Brian that. We should invite him to dinner. Why don't we go bowling with him? Don't you think Brian would like this? How should I know? And how should she, for that matter? It's not like she had seen the guy in years." He chugged his drink and slammed it down. "The guy was a total loser."

Rage rolled off of him. He was more upset that his girlfriend wanted to reconnect with her uncle than he was that she had died. His complete lack of empathy was almost startling. And I couldn't tell if that anger was going to start spilling over into other areas. I glanced at the door as it opened and stood. "I think I see my sister outside. Be right back. I'm going to go check on her."

He didn't even look at me as I backed away from the bar, just motioned for another drink. I scurried through the room, desperately holding on to the mental image of the college girl, and escaped to the sidewalk. My skin felt hot as I power walked to my car, the image slowly slipping from my mind the farther I got from the bar. I held on to it long enough to dip into an empty stairwell before it fell and I became me again.

I walked the rest of my way to my car, my mind buzzing. He had been volatile enough that he might have done it. But the return of a missing uncle also sounded like a promising lead. Maybe I could get justice for Linda after all.

Before heading back to Point Pleasant, I pulled out my phone. While I was in the bar, Betty had texted me.

> **BETTY:**
> Any word from Megan on the results of her testing?

I groaned. I was supposed to bring a sample of Grace's hair to Megan Miller to test to see if she was under the effects of a possession.

DANI:
I haven't been able to get the sample to her yet.

BETTY:
Really? I would have thought you would have by now. It's been a few days.

DANI:
I haven't been able to get it yet.

BETTY:
If you need me to do it, I will.

DANI:
I'll get it done. I'm just waiting for the right opportunity. She's been in her room whenever I'm home.

BETTY:
She isn't still leaving? That's great news.

I sighed. I wish she weren't still leaving. But over the past few days, I could feel Charlie's concern spike whenever she left the house. She didn't pet him anymore.

DANI:
No, it's just been bad timing. She only seems to go out when I'm not home.

BETTY:
You can text me when she leaves, and I'll come right on over.

DANI:
Thanks. I'll keep that in mind. Don't worry, I'll get it done soon, and if I can't, I'll let you know. I promise.

I swallowed the guilt of not collecting the sample right away and focused on the task at hand. Whenever I thought about taking a step back from helping Heather and Izzy figure out what happened to Linda, the headaches came back. If I wanted to figure out what was happening to Grace, I needed to be able to focus on it. The only way out was through. I had to solve one problem before I could move on to the other. Solving the murder was helping Grace.

I closed the conversation with Betty and started a group text with Heather and Izzy.

DANI:
I may have found another lead. You guys game to meet up in the morning for a debrief?

HEATHER:
Breakfast at my place?

IZZY:
Sounds good to me.

DANI:
8 AM?

Both of them sent me a thumbs-up. I stowed my phone and began the long drive home. Construction on I-5 slowed things down.

I mulled over what I'd learned. I had a new name to add to the list of suspects. And if I had to interview Josh again, I wanted to have backup.

CHAPTER 9

The next morning, I arrived at the Bizzy Bean a few minutes early. Charlie had insisted on coming in with me. He was tired of looking after Grace when all she did was wake up and leave the house around noon each day. He was getting antsy at the house alone, and it had been making me less patient. I grabbed his leash, and he scampered across my lap to the ground. For a cat, he had been surprisingly easy to leash train. Maybe that was the perk of his being my familiar. He was brighter than any cat I had ever met, and there were some pretty smart cats out there.

He sauntered ahead of me as I skirted around the building to the back door. I let him in, and he scampered up the stairs to Heather's apartment over the shop. He was a regular visitor and knew the way. I knocked on the front door, and Heather yelled for me to let myself in.

Heather's place had a strange layout. She had torn down walls to make more space for her kitchen, which took up most of the first floor. Her living room and loft bedroom, in comparison, were tiny. There was just enough room for a loveseat. The kitchen really was her pride and joy. A giant island took up the center of the room and had bar seating on one end. An assortment of cast-iron pans lined the wall next to the cabinets. I let Charlie off his leash, and he went off to find the latest round of foster kittens who were too small to move downstairs.

I jumped as my phone rang. I fished it out and answered it.

"Someone broke into my room," Izzy said.

"Are you okay?"

Heather strode around the counter to stand next to me.

"I'm fine. I just... Can you come over?" Izzy's voice cracked.

"Of course." I said goodbye then hung up and explained the situation to Heather.

Charlie darted out the door as I opened it.

"Buddy, where are you going?" I dashed after him.

He ran straight down the stairs and out into the courtyard but stopped at the mudroom door to the bed-and-breakfast. I raised my eyebrow at him. Through the bond we shared, I could feel how focused he was. He stared at the door, willing it to open. I pushed it inward, and he scampered ahead of me, up the rear stairwell to the second floor. He went straight to Izzy's room and batted at the door with his paw until Izzy opened it.

"What on earth are you doing?" I marched out of the stairwell after him.

Charlie pushed past Izzy into her room. She looked down at him, bewildered.

"I'm so sorry," I said. "He's got a mind of his own sometimes."

"It's okay." Izzy took a step back into her room. "I just keep finding other things moved."

I walked into her room, which was a lot like the room Linda had been found in. It had a queen-size bed with an ornate wooden headboard carved with a flower pattern. Bee-themed art filled the walls. And the room looked normal.

Izzy's suitcase sat open at the foot of the bed. Some clothes were slung over the back of a chair, and her laptop was closed on the nightstand.

"Are you sure someone broke in?" I asked as Heather stepped into the room beside me.

"I left my laptop on the other nightstand." Izzy pointed at the computer. "My shirt was on top of my pants. I dropped my socks, but now they're on the chair. And my tape reader was in a different purse pocket. Everything's been moved."

I followed her around the room as she pointed things out. She sank onto the bed, her head in her hands. I stopped next to the nightstand and reached out to brush my fingers along its edge. I fought the urge to yawn. Whoever had touched it last was exhausted.

"I could check the cameras," Heather offered. "I had some installed in the hallways after what happened to Linda."

"I would appreciate that." Izzy hugged her arms to her body.

"What time do you think it happened?" Heather asked as she pulled out her phone.

"I left the room at about seven twenty. I found it just before I called you, so it must have happened sometime in the last thirty minutes."

We crowded around Heather's phone as she played the footage at triple speed. On the screen, Izzy left the room. The hallway remained empty until she returned half an hour later.

"That doesn't make sense. Things moved." Izzy shook her head. "Didn't they? Am I really that tired?"

Her facial expression was so hopeless. My heart broke for her.

"It's okay." I rubbed her shoulder. "You've been through a lot recently. If you need us to come back later, after you've had time to rest, we'll make it work."

"No." Izzy rubbed her eyes. "I really could use the

company. At least, if you're still interested in having breakfast together."

"Of course we still want to do breakfast," Heather said.

"We would never begrudge you for being tired," I added.

"Thank you." Izzy rolled her neck. "Is it all right if I grab a quick shower first? I'm a bit sticky from my run."

I caught Heather's eye. She gave a small nod. We knew each other well. We didn't need to exchange words to know we were both on the same page. Izzy was frazzled and needed us there. While I hadn't known her for long, she was becoming a friend. I couldn't abandon her. And neither could Heather. "Go ahead. We'll wait in here for you if that's okay."

Izzy visibly relaxed at those words. She smiled and ran her hands through her pink hair, then she quickly gathered a change of clothes and ducked into her bathroom.

Once the water started, Heather scurried over to me and whispered, "Is there anything you can do to help her sleep?"

"I have some melatonin at home."

"Not like that. Like..." Heather waggled her fingers at me. "Woogy help."

I tried not to laugh. I had never heard of my magical abilities being described as woogy before. "Not that I know of, but I can ask around."

"I just feel so bad for her." Heather furrowed her brow.

She took a seat in the chair as I paced the room, running my fingers over as many of the items in the space as I could, trying to pick up anything to support Izzy's belief that someone had been in her room. With the security footage, it was doubtful, but I knew from experience cameras couldn't always be relied on. Nor could my psychometry abilities. Neither one was foolproof, but I hadn't found anything that could sneak by both yet, at least without creating something noticeable. The room was filled with anxiety and exhaustion. But there wasn't anything that stood out to me as important. It all felt like how Izzy looked. It didn't seem like there had been anyone else in the room but her.

My fingers were sliding along the handles of the bottom drawer of the dresser when Izzy screamed. I flinched and surged to my feet. Heather beat me to the bathroom door. Steam billowed out as she shoved it open.

Izzy stood in the middle of the small room, her towel wrapped tightly around her, staring at the mirror over the sink. Stark against the fogged-up glass were three words: *He's a liar.*

Charlie pushed his way through my legs, stared at a spot directly behind Izzy, and hissed with his back arched and his fur standing on end.

Izzy spun in place, staring wide-eyed between the glass, Charlie, and the blank space behind her. "What is he looking at?"

The hair on my arms stood up as a cool breeze blew past me. Charlie followed the breeze with his eyes and hissed again. *What was that? Is someone else here?*

"I can't stay here!" Izzy cried.

I swallowed. This was bizarre, even for me. "You can stay with me," I offered.

"You mean that?" Izzy gasped between sobs.

"I've got the space. Let's get you packed up."

Heather sprang into action behind me and pulled Izzy's suitcase onto the bed. I backed out of the bathroom so Izzy could get dressed. She threw on her clothes and came out to help. As Izzy packed, I ducked back into the bathroom. The message was gone from the mirror. I touched the glass. The only emotions I read from it were a mix of exhaustion and boredom. It reminded me of how I felt when I woke up in the morning, when I was still groggy from sleep. I frowned at my reflection. I hadn't imagined the message. But whoever had written it hadn't left an impression. Or they wrote it when they were tired, which made no sense.

I slipped back out into the bedroom and picked up Charlie. Within the minute I'd been in the other room, everything had been shoved into bags and was ready to go. Heather grabbed Izzy's suitcase, while Izzy took her backpack and purse. I led the way down the stairs, with Charlie clutched to my chest. He was still agitated in my grip. I had never felt him so alert before. It was making the hair on my neck stand up and my heart race. I deposited Charlie in the front passenger seat of my car as Izzy and Heather loaded up Izzy's car.

"I am so sorry about this," Heather said again. She had been apologizing profusely for the inconvenience and strange occurrences at the bed-and-breakfast the entire time we packed.

Izzy shook her head. "You don't need to apologize. It's not your fault." Even as she said that, she kept looking over her shoulder at the building.

"Did you want to move the breakfast to my place too?" I asked.

"That's probably a good idea," Heather said. She darted toward the Bizzy Bean. "I'll go grab what I've cooked so far."

After Heather disappeared inside, I stood awkwardly on the sidewalk next to Izzy. The situation at Bee's Bed-and-Breakfast was just plain odd. Maybe because my life had been overtaken by witches, haunted houses, and generational curses, my mind went immediately to the supernatural. There were no signs anyone had broken in, and I had a hard time imagining Izzy writing that on her own mirror. Something else was going on.

The sheriff's SUV pulled up next to me. I stumbled back a few steps as Bob got out of the vehicle and stomped over to me with a scowl on his face. "Haven't I already warned you about meddling in this investigation?"

Izzy stepped up next to me. "She's only here to help me move my stuff."

Bob ignored her and thrust his finger into my face. "I've heard from several people that you are out there asking questions again. You need to back off."

"I—"

"If I hear anything or see anything that makes me think you're sticking your nose where it doesn't belong again, I will haul you in for interfering with a police investigation. Are we clear, Miss Williams?"

I opened my mouth to speak again. "I—"

"I said *are we clear*?" he bellowed.

I nodded.

He turned on his heel and marched back to his vehicle. After slamming his car door shut, he backed out of the parking spot.

I stared at him, slack-jawed, as he drove away.

Izzy exhaled sharply. "Well, that guy isn't a fan of yours."

I gritted my teeth. Bob's dislike of me was really wearing on my nerves. "No, he isn't."

Heather shoved the front door of the Bizzy Bean open. She had a large box in her hands that smelled like bacon and eggs. My stomach rumbled as she carried it toward us. Her eyes flicked between me, Izzy, and the retreating sheriff's car. "Okay. What happened?"

Izzy gave her a quick rundown of the interaction. Her descriptions of his behavior were very colorful. "He was a complete jerk."

"Does that mean you have to stop your investigation?" Heather asked.

"No." I would not let Bob stop me from doing the right thing. He'd had time to prove himself on the last few cases, and I always beat him to the bad guy. I turned to face them. "You ladies ready to head out?"

They both nodded, their eyes wide.

I climbed into the front seat of my car and backed out

into the street. I waited for Izzy to pull up behind me and then led the caravan of cars through town to my place.

Grace's car was still in the driveway, so I had to park on the grass to allow all the vehicles to fit. Charlie led the procession inside. Heather marched into the kitchen and began setting up a breakfast bar for the three of us. She'd brought enough food there to feed a small army. Izzy stood in the middle of the room and turned slowly in place, taking in the surroundings.

"Welcome to my home," I said.

The space was still largely decorated with my grandmother's belongings. I had replaced the faded carpet but hadn't gotten rid of the furniture or various knickknacks that almost overflowed from the shelves lining the back wall. She paused in front of the photo of me, my mother, and Gran over the fireplace. We looked so happy in that photo. I wasn't sure if I could ever take it down, even if my mother had abandoned me. It was the only proof I had that once upon a time, my family had been whole and happy.

A door opened upstairs, and Grace scampered down. "What is that delicious smell?"

"Chocolate chip pancakes." Heather lifted the lid off the last of the containers. "And we'd better dig in soon, before they stop being all melty."

We descended upon the food. Within seconds, we had piled our plates high with scrambled eggs, bacon, and still-steaming pancakes. The insulated carrying case had kept everything warm. Grace joined us at the table. She was covered from head to toe in black. She had a black turtleneck sweater over black leggings and black socks. And to complete the look, she wore black gloves. She sat cross-legged on her chair. I sat with Heather on one side, Grace on the other, and Izzy took the rear corner of the table, her back facing the wall.

"So, what's the occasion?" Grace asked.

I shoved a big mouthful of pancakes into my mouth and chewed it slowly so I would have time to think before I responded. *A murder investigation? Helping a friend through tough times?* I had promised not to hide things from my daughter, as much as possible anyway, so I opted for the truth. "Izzy was staying at Bee's Bed-and-Breakfast while her apartment was getting fixed after a water leak. She found a dead body in what was supposed to be her room and was having a hard time staying there with everything going on around that. So I offered our spare room for a few days while her apartment gets repaired."

Grace's eyes widened, and she almost dropped her fork, but she caught it at the last second and set it down. "I hadn't heard about another body. Who was it?"

"Linda, the winter intern," Heather said.

"She was murdered," Izzy added.

Grace exhaled and shifted in her seat. She shoveled a large forkful of eggs into her mouth. Nodding, she chewed, her eyes bouncing from my face to Heather's then to Izzy's. After almost thirty seconds, she swallowed. "And you're investigating again?"

I nodded.

"Okay." Grace fiddled with her fork. "Well, this goes without saying. But… try to be safe? And I guess, welcome, Izzy. I was about to head out for the day. Did either of you need me to pick up something from the store?"

"No," Izzy and I said in unison.

"Thank you, though," Izzy added.

Grace took a few more bites of food before she stood to clear her plate. She dumped the few remaining bites of pancake into the trash before stopping back at the table to pull me into a hug.

I hugged her back, careful not to accidentally touch any of her exposed skin.

“I love you, Mom.” She kissed me on the top of the head then strode toward the front door.

“Love you too, Pumpkin,” I called after her just before she pulled the front door closed behind her.

I stared at the door. She had seemed so normal again. *Am I imagining that something is wrong? She was so much like her normal self.*

Charlie bumped me with his head, so I scratched it under the table.

“So, status updates?” Heather asked.

“I don’t have much of one.” Izzy pushed a bit of egg around her plate with her fork. “I continued the conversation with Devin after you left, Dani. He was wound pretty tight after all those questions we asked. The only way to get him to open up again was to not ask anything. It’s clear to me he’s hiding something. I just don’t know what. But I was able to schedule a follow-up interview with him.”

“He agreed to an interview?” I asked.

Izzy smiled sheepishly. “More like agreed to a date.”

I straightened in my chair and put my hand on her arm. “Are you sure that’s safe?”

“I made certain it would be in a public place. And I promise…” She held up three fingers. “That I will keep you both on speed dial in case anything goes wrong.”

“Good. I wish I could say my conversation with the boyfriend, Josh, was productive.” I relaxed again as I gave them an update on his anger issues and the lead he had given me on Linda’s uncle.

“I wonder if he’s the liar,” Heather said.

My mind flashed to that cryptic message that had been drawn in the fog on Izzy’s mirror. “I don’t know,” I admitted

Izzy squirmed. “I don’t want to think about that. At least not yet.”

“Did he give any useful information on who this uncle is?” Heather asked, changing the subject.

"Just a first name. Brian."

We all pulled out our phones and began poking around to find out what Brian was like. We found his full name on Linda's page. They shared a last name, Cartwright, so it wasn't hard to track down more information once we had that. With each new discovery, we shared it over breakfast. Heather found his current employer, a construction company named Walsh Masonry and Concrete, based out of Anacortes. I recognized the name. I had worked with them on a couple of claims. Izzy confirmed he was the older brother of Linda's father, who'd passed away when Linda was eight.

Josh had mentioned he disappeared from Linda's life years ago, so I spent my time poking around her mother's social media. He was right. Brian was in tons of family photos until right before Linda's tenth birthday, then he was just gone. *But what would take him out of her life like that?* I couldn't find a sign of him anywhere after her tenth birthday until I pulled up the Island County court records.

I slumped into my seat, my eyes still focused on my screen.

"What is it?" Heather asked.

Eight years ago, he had been found guilty of driving a stolen vehicle, assault and battery, possession of an unlicensed firearm, amongst a wide assortment of drug-related charges. Brian Cartwright hadn't just walked out of Linda's life. He had been marched out of it by the justice system.

"Brian Cartwright is a convicted felon," I said at last. "And I need to interview him."

CHAPTER 10

We spent the next hour bickering over what to do next. Izzy didn't feel comfortable with me interviewing someone with a history of violence by myself. I wasn't sure about Izzy interviewing Devin alone either. Heather thought we were both being ridiculous and urged us to tell Chris about our suspicions. Neither Izzy nor I wanted to do that. The pressure at the back of my head kept telling me I needed to investigate. And Izzy just said no. I wouldn't fight her on the one-word response since she was agreeing with me. After an hour of back-and-forth negotiations, we ended the conversation where it had begun: Izzy would interview Devin on their *date,* I would interview Brian, and Heather would remain the voice of reason when we got back from fumbling around with our harebrained ideas. With that, Heather left to go back to work, and Izzy went down to the daylight basement to finally catch some shuteye, leaving me alone in the kitchen.

I mentally went through the list of things I had to get accomplished that day. Surprisingly, I was all caught up at work, so unless a time-sensitive claim came in, I could take the day off. With everything else on my plate, it was an attractive option. But with an entirely free day ahead of me, I was frozen with indecision. I glanced out the kitchen window. My car was still parked on the grass, but Heather and Grace had left, leaving only Izzy in the actual driveway. *Grace.* I had promised Betty I would get a sample of her hair for Megan Miller, and I was finally home when she wasn't. Now might be the only time to do it.

I gathered my maps from under the coffee table and quickly cast a tracking spell to locate Grace's car. It was parked at the same trailhead she had been parked at the last time I looked for her. *She could be hiking. Couldn't she?* I chewed on my lip. The only way to know was to track Grace herself. While tracking spells didn't work on a person very well, I could try to find the sweater she had been wearing when she left the house.

My hands shook as I searched for a picture of her wearing the sweater. I knew her car well enough I could cast the spell without a visual aid, but focusing on the image of a sweater was harder. I found a good photo and cast the tracking spell a second time. The lights were slower to settle than when I was looking for her car, but they did eventually. Grace was at Meredith Walker's house.

I felt as if the wind had gone out of my sails. She had no reason to go there alone—not one I understood, at least. Something was wrong with my daughter.

My legs shook as I fetched a pair of latex gloves from my adjuster kit. The shaking continued into my hands as I slid them into place. Knowing that spying on my daughter was the right choice didn't help. I shuffled into her bathroom. Sitting on the counter was her hairbrush. I pulled a few strands from the center and deposited them in a ziplock baggie. With my task completed, I put the brush back where I'd found it and scurried to my car before I lost my nerve. Charlie scampered after me, refusing to be left behind.

I drove on autopilot through the intersection that led up

to Miller's farm. I didn't have a good phone number for Megan, but she hardly ever left her house, so I wasn't worried she wouldn't be there. Part of me hoped she wouldn't be so that I could put off knowing what was wrong with Grace a little longer. Whenever I contemplated turning back, Charlie chirped next to me, encouraging me to keep going. He stood on his back legs and stared out the window as we drove up the long, winding driveway to Megan's place.

Megan's truck was parked in the driveway. I trudged up to her front door and raised my hand to knock, but then I heard her voice coming out of the open barn door. The barn sat kitty-corner to the home. It was made of wood, its red paint peeling where someone had egged it. I followed the sound and found her milking the cow that had stood at the house window. It was no longer painted purple. Up close, the thing was massive. She was a black-and-white dairy cow, except she was almost six feet tall at the shoulders. She mooed when she noticed me standing in the doorway.

"I wondered when you were going to come by," Megan said without turning around.

"I would have called, but…"

"Gertie, this is Dani. Dani, this is Gertie. And who do you have with you?" Megan finished milking, stood, and patted Gertie's haunches.

"His name is Charlie."

"He's a beaut." Megan beamed at him. Her smile brightened her face. It was so joyful. "What's it like having a cat for a familiar?"

I blinked. *How does she know?* I suppose it made sense, since I'd shown up with a cat off leash. "It's been wonderful."

"I love my Gertie, but I have to admit I sometimes wish my familiar were a tad more portable. Not that I travel much, but the number of places I can take a cow is limited." Megan chuckled as she walked past me. "You want some coffee?"

"Sure." I followed her into her house.

Gertie took up her position at the kitchen window. Charlie hopped onto the windowsill and rubbed his head against hers. He then sat down and stared into Gertie's eyes.

"What are they doing?" I asked.

"Getting to know each other." Megan put the kettle on the stove. "Now, I don't need to have divination powers to know something's bothering you."

Shifting in my seat, I ducked my head. I tried hard not to wear my emotions on my sleeve, but the stress had been getting to me. My shoulders were raised higher than usual, and whenever I closed my mouth, my teeth clenched together. I hadn't realized how bad it was until I tried to relax, and my jaw ached as I stretched it out. "Maybe a little," I admitted. "It feels like my life exploded when I found out I'm a witch, and it just keeps getting worse every time I turn around."

"Do you need a sympathetic ear, advice, comfort, or something else?"

I laughed. "All of the above sounds good."

Megan poured me a cup of coffee and took a seat opposite me at the kitchen table. She sipped at her coffee and motioned for me to speak.

Once the floodgates opened, I word vomited everything that was wrong in my life in a barely coherent rant. "Where do I even start? My daughter, Grace, might be possessed or mind controlled by the witch who cursed our entire family. My relationship with Chris is a disaster. We had just become an official couple, and I messed it all up by not telling him about Abby. But what was I supposed to do? Abby wasn't guilty, and the real killer was using magic to hide his trail. And now, I'm involved in another investigation. Which I'm sure he's upset about, but I can't not investigate because whenever I even think about not investigating, I get splitting headaches. Bob has tried to scare me away from it already, so I know Chris knows. It's awful. It's all awful. And the investigation isn't going great. My friend Izzy is so exhausted from lack of sleep that she's half sick, distracted by random sounds, and convinced someone keeps moving her stuff. But no one has, at least as far as I can feel when I touch the items. And now, she's at my house. In the same house as Grace. I don't know why I invited her. It just came out of me when she was crying about a creepy message on her bathroom mirror. But what if Grace is possessed and does something to her as well?"

With each word, Megan's eyes got slightly wider behind the rim of her mug.

I slumped in my chair, exhausted. "So I guess not much is wrong at all. Right?" I tried to laugh my outburst off, but it came out sounding too forced.

Megan put down her mug and caught my eye. "You're a wonderful mother who cares about her daughter. You are doing everything you can to figure out what's wrong with her. Now, are you ready for some advice?"

I nodded and ducked my head, peering at her through a curtain of my hair.

"Come clean to Chris—"

I sat bolt upright. "I can't—"

Megan held up a finger.

I clamped my mouth shut and collapsed back into my seat.

Megan kept her finger up for a few more seconds before lowering her hand and continuing. "Come clean to Chris. He's one of the few people I talk to, and half those conversations are about you. He's crazy about you. And I am sure he will understand. Now, for this murder investigation… How is your friend Izzy involved?"

"She found the body."

Megan nodded. "I thought so. Have you checked to see if she is being haunted?"

"I… How do you check for something like that?"

Megan winced. "It really is easier with a necromancer, but a séance can work in a pinch if you don't have one available. They're not foolproof, but it's better than nothing."

"A séance? Like with a Ouija board?"

"Historically, there was one involved, but there are easier ways to communicate now with the marvels of modern technology." Megan stood and grabbed a pad of paper and a pen from a drawer. "I can give you some directions if that will help."

"That would be amazing," I said.

"You'll have to do this soon. Spirits only really hang out until the next full moon, unless there is something holding them here. Injustice might. I wouldn't want to bet on it." Megan began jotting things down. "Now, did you bring the sample we talked about?"

I nodded and pulled out the baggie of Grace's hair. "It's right here."

She exchanged her notes on how to perform a séance with the plastic bag. Her handwriting was messy but legible enough. It was written more like a recipe than any of the spells my grandmother had described. It was practical and simplistic in its directions.

"Thank you for doing this," I said. "I… I'm sorry I was so awful to you when we first met."

"It was the curse." Megan waved me off.

"That explains my behavior, but it doesn't excuse it." I folded the séance directions and put them into my pocket. "I hope it isn't too late for us to be friends."

"I would love to be friends. Oh, before I forget, I have something for you." Megan stood and darted toward the other room.

A few seconds later, she emerged with a package in her hands. It had a familiar shape and wrapping. It looked exactly like the ones that had arrived from my mysterious benefactor with notebooks left by my gran. In the same neat script as the other packages was my name: Dani Williams.

"What's that?" My breath caught in my throat.

"Not sure," she said. "It arrived on my doorstep this morning."

I swallowed as I took it from her, my hands shaking. The strongest emotion on the package was curiosity. She really didn't know what it was. I slowly unwrapped the brown paper.

"Is that what I think it is?" Megan asked.

"A spell book from my gran."

She moved her chair around the table to sit next to me, and we flipped through the book together. It was her specialty—enchantments. She helped me read through each of the sections and even filled in a few gaps. She told me how it was easier to call on someone's worst impulses than appeal to their better natures. As we flipped to the last page, my gaze landed on the words *6 of 7*. My eyes watered. I was getting close to the end of my gran's instructions. Soon, that connection would be gone.

"Are you okay?" Megan asked.

I nodded. "It's strange holding onto my gran's notebooks."

"Isn't having something like this a good thing?"

I wiped my eyes. "Yeah. It's just there's only one more after this, and… I usually celebrate with my daughter."

Megan patted my hand. "Once we get this thing with Grace sorted, you'll get to celebrate with her again."

"Are you sure?"

She nodded. I could feel her uncertainty through the table. I chose to ignore it and focus on her words instead. Grace was going to be okay.

CHAPTER 11

I pulled up in front of a large brick home in Oak Harbor. Scaffolding had been erected on one side of the house, with plastic covering large sections of the wall to keep out the rain as the brickwork was being redone. On the other side, a retaining wall was being constructed. The sounds of hammering in the backyard indicated there was a third team on site. It was an overcast day, with storm clouds forming in the distance.

I rechecked the name of the foreman I had gotten from Cindy Walsh, the owner of Walsh Masonry. She had been more than happy to let me talk to one of their foremen about a potential project for the city. And the foreman just so happened to be overseeing the same job site Brian Cartwright worked at. It had taken a bit of finagling to make sure I got the right one. I had called to set up a meeting just before they all broke for lunch to maximize my chances of getting a one-on-one conversation with Linda's mysterious uncle.

The foreman wasn't hard to find. He was standing at the back of his pickup truck with a set of plans laid flat in the bed, poring over them as he jotted down notes on a clipboard. He wore an orange hard hat, mud-splattered blue jeans, and a long-sleeve flannel shirt. An assortment of tools hung from his belt. I recognized him from a claim I'd handled a few months back. The poor homeowner had an addition built onto their house by another contractor, but it had settled unevenly, and their chimney stack had separated from the side of the home. Luckily, Walsh could fix the problem. They did good work.

"Jose Ramos?" I asked as he put the clipboard under his arm.

He turned, his expression shifting from inquisitive to happy in an instant. A wide smile spread across his face as he stepped forward, hand outstretched to shake mine. "Dani! Long time no see. Miss Walsh said you'd be coming by today. What can I do for you?"

"I've been roped into a restoration project for the Point Pleasant City Council. We're hoping to get the old sheriff's station back up and running."

He nodded. "It's a crime that it's taken so long. A water leak shouldn't shutter a place like that for this long. Five years. It's shameful. So what do you need from me?"

"I haven't been inside yet, but just from what I've seen through the windows, I know we're going to have to do some masonry work. Could you explain some of what you do? I want to be able to make some more informed recommendations to the council when they meet about it."

"Of course." He put his thumbs into his belt loops and rocked back on his heels. "I'm always happy to help. But you know I'd be able to explain things better if we were there in person."

I laughed. "Don't worry. There will be time for that. But could you humor me in the meantime?"

I grabbed my hard hat from my home inspection kit and followed him around the job site. He was quick and efficient, explaining things well as we went from area to area. We spent the most time up the scaffolding, looking at the brick repair work that was being completed. It was one of those things where everything sounded simple, but doing it was a lot more complicated. As we walked, I took a peek at every worker we passed, trying to find Brian in the mix. I had begun to lose hope that he had come in to work that day when we turned the corner to the backyard, and I saw him building an outdoor kitchen.

Brian wasn't much older than me. He was ruggedly handsome, with a hint of gray at his temples. He was kneeling next to a half-completed brick wall, with a trowel in one hand and a brick in the other.

Bringing things up casually was a skill I only sometimes excelled at. It was so much easier over the phone than in person. Clearing my throat, I cocked my head in Brian's direction. "Is that Brian Cartwright?" I asked Jose.

He paused in his explanation of appropriate temperatures to do brickwork, his expression shifting to somber. Jose had one of the most expressive faces I'd ever seen. "I told him he didn't need to come in today, but he's being a trouper."

"I knew Linda. Would it be okay if I give him my condolences when we're done?"

He nodded and launched right back into his explanation. "You want it to be at least forty degrees, or it just won't cure properly."

I kept Brian in view as we finished up the tour. The trip really had been helpful for the restoration project. I hoped Walsh would put in a competitive bid for the work, because it would be nice to work with them on it. After we finished, Jose shook my hand and strode back to his truck to finish his logs before going to lunch, and I wandered over to say hello to one of my suspects.

"Brian?" I asked softly. "Brian Cartwright?"

He put down his trowel and stood, wiping his hands on his jeans. "That's me."

"Hi." I held out my hand. "I'm Dani Williams."

He eyed it before shaking. "What can I do for you?"

I studied his eyes as I stepped closer. They were green. I tried not to sigh. Green eyes should have helped narrow down the suspect pool, but all three of the men on my list had them. I softened my expression. "I wanted to extend my condolences. Linda was such a sweetheart. I understand you two were pretty close."

He stiffened and looked away. "I wouldn't go so far as to say that."

"Oh? The way she talked about you, I would have assumed you two were as thick as thieves. Last time I saw her, she was excited about dinner plans or something like that."

He wouldn't look at me, stepping back to lean against the finished portion of the kitchen wall. "She was a good kid."

I moved next to him and rested my hand on the wall. My stomach fluttered as the bottom of it dropped out. The muscles in my arms quivered, and my mouth went dry. He was nervous about something. I studied him. He stood with his arms crossed and his eyes averted, the body language of someone who was hiding something. And the nervousness I picked up from the wall all but confirmed it.

"I just can't believe it," I said. "I can't imagine why anyone would want to hurt her."

My chest tightened, and pain hit the back of my throat. *Guilt?*

"I don't know why either, lady." He pushed himself away from the wall.

Inwardly, I sighed at the lost contact. The last emotion I had picked up from him was guilt. *But is he still feeling guilty? What is he hiding?* Unfortunately, he wasn't eating anything for me to cast a relaxation potion spell on. I would have to interview him the old-fashioned way. He was walking away, so I took a gamble. "If you know something that would help catch whoever did this, you should tell someone."

He spun, nostrils flaring, and stomped toward me. "I don't know who you think you are—"

I stepped back and held up my hands, palms facing outward. "I'm just a friend of a friend expressing concern."

He thrust his finger into my face. "I don't need any more friends. So leave me out of whatever grief fetish you have going on."

Before I could respond, he turned on his heel and stormed away. My hands dropped to my sides as I stared after him. His coworkers rounded the building and looked between the two of us. They gathered in a large cluster and whispered to one another. The hairs on the back of my neck stood up as they stared at me. I hunched my shoulders, shoved my hands into my pockets, and stalked back to my car.

Brian marched to his vehicle ahead of me and slammed his car door shut behind him. My eyes flicked between him and the other workers, who had their eyes trained on me. Going after him would be a bad look, so I pulled out my phone and took a surreptitious photo of his car. If I couldn't talk to him at the moment, I would at least be able to track him down later. I shoved the phone into my pocket, climbed into my own car, and left before I attracted any more attention.

CHAPTER 12

I was becoming as bad as Izzy and Grace about sleeping, tossing and turning all night. I couldn't remember my dreams upon waking, but by the hammering of my heart and the sweat drenching my body, a scream half formed in my throat, I knew they weren't good. Everything around the house was slipping. The sink was full of dishes, and I hadn't vacuumed in days. Charlie's fur clung to the carpet and covered half my clothes. I felt like a terrible host. Poor Izzy was probably regretting her decision to stay at my house. I ended up oversleeping and, in my haste, forgot my lunch. By noon, my brain was too foggy to focus on work, and my stomach demanded food, so I locked up early and headed to the Slice of Life diner on my way home.

Parking around the diner was sparse, but I found a spot three blocks away and walked over. It would have been faster to walk from my office. The only perk about walking from a different direction than usual was I got to see the spread of the art going up around town. John Porter had put a stained-glass sculpture in the park, and a mural had been spray-painted on another bus stop. That one was of a stunning waterfall, with purple fog-like clouds around it.

I could smell the diner before I got to it. The scent of brownies and hot spiced apples filled the air as I approached. My stomach rumbled with each step. I followed my nose inside and walked up to the counter to put in a to-go order. Willow was at the register. She had her hair in a braided circlet around her head and wore her usual red-rimmed glasses and a flowing teal-and-green maxi dress.

"What will it be?" she asked as I stepped in front of her.

I studied the menu above her head. She had added some of Abby's creations. My eyes bounced from section to section. It all sounded delicious. "Could I get the zuppa Toscana soup with cheesy bread and an apple tart?"

She smiled. "Coming right up."

I stepped aside so the next customer in line could put in their order and scanned the dining area to find a place to sit. My gaze landed on Stacey Holmes and Mason Grant, two of the bed-and-breakfast guests, sitting together in one of the rear booths. Willow had decorated the diner with photos of the town through the decades, organized by season. The section they were sitting in celebrated summer in Point Pleasant. Each picture had vibrant colors and laughing faces.

I chewed on my lip. They were on my short list of potential witnesses. *I wonder if they saw Josh or Brian hanging around the bed-and-breakfast before the murder.* It didn't hurt to ask, so I caught Stacey's eye and waved. She waved back. I took that as an invitation and walked over to their table.

"Fancy seeing you here," I said. "Have you eaten here before? It's the best food in town."

"That's what I heard." Stacey motioned for me to sit. "Everything I've had in town so far has been wonderful. And it's a good thing too. With this investigation going on, I thought it was only right to stick around a little longer in case the sheriff needed to talk to me again. And the food is making it a much more enjoyable experience."

As she talked, Stacey casually touched Mason's arm and

pointed at the menu. It seemed she wasn't staying in town just for the food. The company looked good too.

"If you're willing to help out, would you mind if I asked you a few more questions myself?" I asked.

"Why not?" Stacey beamed.

Mason shrugged and put down his menu.

I showed them the picture of Josh that I had taken at the bar. "Do either of you recognize this man?"

Stacey pulled a pair of reading glasses from her purse and squinted at my phone. I leaned forward so she could get a closer look.

"I don't think so," she said.

Mason glanced at the image and shook his head. "Doesn't look familiar to me either."

I sighed and pulled up a picture of Brian. "How about this guy?"

"Maybe?" Stacey said.

Mason leaned forward to study the photo. "Who are they?"

"I guess you could call them people of interest. At least to me."

"Can I see them both again?" Mason asked.

I flipped between the two photos. He nodded when I flipped back to the photo of Brian. "I couldn't tell at first, but he looks an awful lot like a guy I saw having some sort of argument with a girl. I didn't get a great look at her, though."

My heart skipped a beat, and I slid forward. I fumbled with my phone to find a picture of Linda and showed it to him. "Was it her?"

"I think so."

"Dani!" Willow called.

I glanced over at the counter. She had my order wrapped up, ready to go. I slid out of the booth. "Thank you for your time."

I had a bounce in my step as I collected my food and

walked back to my car, and I barely noticed it had started sprinkling again. Mason had given me an eyewitness account of Brian having an argument with the victim, so Brian moved up my list of suspects. He and Josh were tied for the top place.

I couldn't stop thinking about the two suspects as I drove home. Both of them had green eyes, like the killer, and seemed to have violent tendencies. And they were both hiding something.

As I pulled into my driveway, my focus on the case faltered. Grace's car was gone. I knew where I would find her car if I went looking. Hanging my head, I shuffled into the house.

Charlie greeted me at the door, swishing his tail impatiently, and he yowled at me as if to object to being left at home again. I scooped him up and carried him into the kitchen, where I snagged him a few treats and tossed them into his food bowl before I took a seat at the table. He sniffed at the treats and opted to forgive me for my misdeeds.

As I ate, I chatted to him about the case. It helped to say things out loud sometimes, and he was always a good listener. I finished up lunch as I talked and moved on to cleaning up the house. He followed me around as I worked, chirping occasionally as I spitballed ideas. I kept getting the sense that I was missing something important. The longer I ruminated, the more certain I became.

"Do you think I should make an anonymous tip to the sheriff's department about what Mason saw? Maybe they could—" I winced as the pressure in my head spiked in warning. I doubled over and tried to blink away black spots.

Charlie darted toward me and peered up into my face.

I closed my eyes and exhaled slowly through my mouth. I had been about to suggest handing off the investigation to them. My legs shook as I sank to my knees. There was no handing this one off. I pinched the bridge of my nose. "I'm all right, buddy."

I sighed. It was weak evidence. They probably wouldn't do anything with it anyway. I would need to take them something bigger if I wanted it to stick. *But what?* I pushed myself up, stalked over to my purse, and pulled out the new notebook from my gran. I had been so busy with the investigation that I hadn't had time to study any of the spells yet. Most of them made me a little uneasy. Almost every spell had a big, bolded warning next to it saying to use them with caution. They were spells about influencing people's emotions or making it so people would forget the details of a conversation. I was flipping past the spell on charming a person when Megan's instructions for a séance fell out.

I crouched down to pick them up. The hair on the back of my neck stood up. I paused and closed my eyes. I ran my finger along the piece of paper and focused on my body. *Should I perform a séance?* The hair on my arms and neck stood up. It was a clear yes.

A séance required either a necromancer or three witches. I didn't know any necromancers, but I knew where I could find two other witches, so I dialed the Retirees and told them to meet me at the Bizzy Bean in half an hour. Before they could ask any questions, I hung up. I kissed Charlie on top of his head and marched out to my car.

Despite my gruff invitation, when I strode into the café, they were seated at their usual table, waiting for me.

I shuffled my way into the plexiglass enclosure and gave them a sheepish smile in apology. "Thank you for coming."

"Did you get Grace's results from Megan?" Betty leaned forward, hope in her eyes.

"No, I called you here about something else." I hovered over the table.

Betty snorted, crossed her arms, and looked away, muttering. "What could be more important than that?"

Agnes elbowed her and returned my smile. "You look tired, dear. Are you doing okay?"

I sighed and took a seat across from them. They had sat in a line on one side of the table. It felt like I was being interviewed, the way the three of them looked at me. I shifted in my seat and cleared my throat. "I need your help with performing a séance."

They exchanged a look with each other. Normally, they had a habit of talking over one another, but now, they were all quiet. When they silently communicated, it was somehow worse. It made my ask feel big, even though in theory, it was a simple spell.

"A séance for who?" Sarah broke the silence after almost a full minute.

"Linda," I said. "The B&B maid who died."

They visibly relaxed.

"Oh, you're investigating another murder, are you?" Agnes asked.

Betty still hadn't spoken. Her arms were crossed, and she was glowering at me.

Was I really that rude when I called? The exhaustion must be getting to me. I'll have to do something to make it up to her. Blushing under the weight of their gazes, I shifted in my seat again. "I am."

"Don't you think you should be focused on other things?" Betty leaned forward and jabbed her finger into the wood of the table. "The haunted house? Your daughter? This curse situation. You're beginning to seem a lot like—"

"It's probably a good thing she has something to keep her distracted," Agnes cut in.

"A lot like who?" I asked. My face flushed. I didn't need her to say it. I knew who she was going to say. "My mother?"

How dare she compare me to my mother? This was different. My mom left me for months at a time with no warning when I was growing up. The Retirees knew it wasn't the same. They had picked me up countless times from the bus stop when I had to come up to my Gran's when I ran out of food after my mother left unexpectedly. I was just a child. They held me while I cried, wondering why my mother didn't want me. It was not like I had abandoned my daughter. I *was* here for her. I *was* fighting for her. *I'm nothing like Lori.*

"Dani—" Sarah put her hand on Betty's shoulder.

My blood boiled as I surged to my feet. "You think I don't want to focus on that? But the Sight won't let me. If I do anything but investigate, I get crippling headaches. They are so bad I can barely stand. How can you expect me to help my daughter if I'm a puddle on the floor?"

They leaned back in their chairs in unison, their eyes wide.

"Can you help me or not?" I gritted my teeth.

"I've never done a séance before." Sarah looked back and forth between Betty and Agnes. I was willing to bet if she hadn't done one, neither had they. They had been in a coven together since high school.

"I wouldn't even know where to start," Agnes said.

"That's okay." I pulled out the directions I had gotten from Megan and slapped them down on the table. "I know how. It's supposedly easiest if you're a necromancer, but if you're not, then it requires three witches to do."

"Three?" Betty asked.

I nodded and slid the piece of paper across the table to her. "A necromancer has such a strong connection to death that they can represent all three sides of a person at once. But when the connection is weaker, you need a witch for all three sides: the mind, the body, and the soul. And you have to do it quickly. You only have until the next full moon, then it doesn't work anymore. Not without a necromancer performing the spell."

"Where did you get this?" Betty handed the paper to Agnes so she could read it next.

"Megan. I was thinking, Agnes, you could represent the mind." I held up my hand and ticked them off. "Betty, you can represent the body, and I can represent the soul."

"Are you sure that's wise?" Betty asked. "My curse might mess it up."

"I'll guide the spell. We've cast things together before. My taking the lead should mitigate those risks." I held her gaze as Agnes handed the spell down the line to Sarah.

"But this is… necromancy." Betty squirmed.

"It's a séance. It's not like I'm raising the dead."

I watched them discuss it. They were talking over one another again, so I couldn't make heads or tails out of their conversation, but somehow, they always kept track of the thread.

"It says you need an object of the deceased." Sarah handed the page back to me.

I turned and motioned Heather over. "Do you still have anything of Linda's? We need a personal object to perform a séance."

She nodded. "She left a few things in her locker. I still have her favorite coffee mug and a pair of shoes."

I swiveled back to the Retirees. "The coffee mug should work, right?"

They shrugged in unison.

"It's new territory for me," Agnes said.

"If it doesn't work, then it doesn't work. But at least we tried something." I held my breath, waiting for them to respond.

Agnes slumped first. Betty glared at her and crossed her arms.

Sarah looked between the two of them and back at me. She was so often the deciding vote. "They'll do it."

"What?" Betty spluttered.

"It's the right thing to do," Sarah said.

"Fine." Betty snatched the spell back from me and read it a second time. "So, when are we going to do this thing?"

"I was thinking now." I forced a smile onto my face to try to ease some of the tension.

Betty handed the spell back to me. Heather peered over my shoulder, reading it. "I have most of the ingredients already. Let's do this."

Betty frowned. "This is witches' business."

Heather crossed her arms. "It's my building, and I have the supplies. Plus, I'm the one who knew Linda best. I should be involved."

"All right," Betty said. "But I don't like it."

CHAPTER 13

I stepped away from the table. *Did I go too far? Am I being like my mother?* I clamped down on the doubt. I needed to do the séance so I could put this case behind me and focus on my daughter. *The Retirees will understand. Won't they?* I knew them. The answer was yes, but that didn't mean how I was acting was okay. *Shoot. I'm going to owe them a serious apology after this.*

Betty glowered at me for a second longer before standing and following me to Bee's Bed-and-Breakfast next door. Heather darted into a side room to collect supplies while the rest of us marched up the stairs to the second floor. We gathered around the door to the room where Linda's body had been discovered. I still wasn't sure where the crime had actually occurred, and there had been too much foot traffic through the area for me to figure it out. There was still crime scene tape on the door.

"Should we be going in there?" Sarah asked.

"The sheriff cleared it yesterday. They just were waiting for the biohazard cleanup company to come through before removing the tape." Heather stepped onto the landing, her arms around a bundle of stuff wrapped in a tarp.

Agnes blanched. "How bad is it in there?"

I pushed the door open. The room was dark but exactly how I had left it. If we didn't know it was a crime scene, it would have looked like a normal bedroom. I ducked under the tape and went inside. The Retirees followed, and Heather took up the rear, shutting the door behind her.

"So, what's the tarp for?" I asked as Heather unpacked.

"The spell called for a ring of salt." Heather laid the tarp down on the floor. "I didn't want to get it all over the carpet."

Heather was always so practical. I smiled and helped her set up. We put a candle down on each corner of the tarp then sprinkled a circle of salt connecting them. Next, Heather put a speaker in the center of the circle. Ouija boards worked but were slow. According to Megan's notes, ghosts could access speakers and speak to us through them when called. I wasn't sure how I felt about hearing a dead woman speak, but I needed answers, and this was the best way to get them.

Heather took up a position on the bed, and I stepped into the salt circle, motioning for Betty and Agnes to join me. They moved inside, leaving Sarah alone near the door. She wrung her hands, staring at her friends. I couldn't imagine how frustrating it would be to only be able to cast magic on the full moon. At the moment, she was powerless, and she couldn't even give her coven the emotional support she usually did during times like these.

I sat the spell page down on top of the speaker so I could still read it and reached out my hands. Betty took the right and Agnes the left. We formed a circle around the speaker.

"Are you ready?" I asked.

They both nodded.

Heather pulled out her phone. "Remember, you will only have a minute to ask questions. I'm going to start a timer once she arrives."

I cleared my throat and began the chant. Motes of golden light swirled out of me and danced along the salt line. The candlelight flared and swayed as if buffeted by wind. Agnes picked up the chant next, melding her words with mine. As she spoke, an incandescent glow filled the space around us. The salt line confined our magic to the space and concentrated it, giving it more power. Betty joined in last. Her words were shaky at first but grew in confidence as she successfully funneled her power into me. Her misshapen pearly orbs danced around the space, mingling with my motes of light until there was a pillar of light in the middle of the room. As the spell came to an end, I said the final words: "Linda Cartwright, we call to you."

I flinched as the speaker squealed to life. Heather held up her phone to show the timer.

The static faded, and a voice came through. "Where am I?"

"Linda?" I asked.

"Yes?" Her voice was small and frightened.

"We need to know who attacked you," I said.

"I didn't see…" Linda sobbed. "Where am I?"

My heart sank. I glanced at the timer. Ten seconds gone. "Do you have any idea who it could have been? Was it Josh?"

"It couldn't have been," Linda said. "I had just FaceTimed him. He was in Seattle. Did someone kill me?"

"I'm so sorry." A tear slid down Agnes's face. "You poor girl."

I squeezed Agnes's hand. "Linda, I need you to focus. Had anyone threatened you?"

"Is that why that pink-haired woman keeps ignoring me?" Linda was more focused, just on the wrong thing.

I glanced at the clock. Thirty-five seconds gone. "Please, Linda. We don't have long. Did anyone want to hurt you?"

"It's really rude of her. You shouldn't just ignore people." Linda continued like I hadn't said anything. "Why won't she just talk to me?"

"Linda, please." I tried to keep the frustration out of my voice. "Would Brian have hurt you?"

"Brian? He—"

The time hit one minute, and her voice disappeared mid-sentence.

I cursed under my breath. The light faded, leaving us in a dimly lit room.

"Can we try again?" Betty whispered.

"No." I hung my head.

Heather slid off the bed. "Well… you at least got one suspect off your list. That's good, right?"

"I suppose." I slumped forward, my shoulders rounding inward as I hugged my arms to my body. "But I still have two other suspects. I was really hoping to get this one solved so I could focus on personal stuff."

The Retirees moved in and put their hands on my shoulders. We stood there in silence as they funneled sympathy and understanding into me. I had been curt with them, but they were still there for me. I reached up and squeezed their hands in thanks.

"I just don't understand why she was so focused on Izzy, you know?" I slumped onto the bed. "Is it possible for regular people to hear ghosts?"

"Usually, the only people who hear them are necromancers or mediums," Betty said.

Sarah picked up where Betty had left off. "But if the ghost is strong enough, sometimes, they can break through on their own."

"Hence haunted houses. Not everyone who lives in one is a medium," Agnes finished.

"What's a medium?" Heather asked.

"They're witch adjacent. Like us, they're born that way," Betty began.

And just like before, Sarah continued. "But they can't cast spells."

"By their very nature, they either go crazy from hearing all the voices, or they figure it out," Agnes said.

"There really isn't an in between," Betty added.

Sarah started, "All mediums either know exactly what they are..."

"Or they end up in an asylum because no amount of medication can help." Agnes sighed. "It really is a sad condition."

"So, if Izzy were one, she would know?" I asked.

"By now?" The Retirees exchanged looks before Betty answered. "Most definitely."

I mulled that over. I had never discussed anything mystical with Izzy, so I didn't know what her thoughts were on that topic. But I had never noticed her acting odd before, and we had been at murder scenes together in the past. Linda had left a message on the mirror. Maybe she was just a very strong ghost.

After a minute, the Retirees filtered out of the room to give me space.

Heather wrapped her arms around me and pulled me into a hug. "Two more suspects isn't bad. Devin and Brian, right?"

I nodded.

"Have you talked to Chris about it yet? He might know something," Heather said.

I stiffened. "He still isn't talking to me."

"Oh, Dani." Heather hugged me again. "I know you probably don't want to hear it, but maybe you need to take a leap of faith and tell him the truth."

"Not you too." I grimaced and wiped at my face.

She barked out a nervous laugh. "How many people are giving you that advice?"

"Betty. Agnes. Sarah. Grace. Megan. And now you." I paced as I went through the list of names, my heart pounding in my ears. Everyone was piling on with the same advice. But none of them had to have that conversation with Chris. None of them had to face losing someone they loved.

Heather furrowed her brow. "Who's Megan?"

I winced. I hadn't been thinking straight when I said her name. Only a few days into knowing somebody else's secret, and I had already spilled the beans. "Megan Miller."

Heather recoiled and crossed her arms. "Well, maybe it isn't good advice then. Not if *she's* giving it."

"Do you have any coffee?" I asked.

"Always, but now's not the time." Heather put her hands on her hips.

"Trust me. It is."

Heather snorted and walked out of the room. "I have some in the foyer downstairs."

I followed her out. When we got to the coffeepot, I quickly cast the spell I had witnessed Megan use twice to clear someone's thoughts. I poured Heather a cup and handed her the mug. "Drink this?"

Heather's eyebrow rose, and she took a sip. Her eyes widened, and she stared at me. "Why was I just thinking horrible things about a woman I've never met?"

I motioned for her to follow me back upstairs. We had to clean up the ritual space, anyway, and I didn't want anyone else to overhear our conversation. When we were back in the room, I closed the door behind us. "You know how my family is cursed?"

She nodded.

"Well, Megan's family is also cursed. Except hers is even nastier in a way. It makes people inherently distrust her."

Heather covered her mouth with her hand. "I owe that woman a mountain of cookies."

"You can't tell anyone," I said.

"Of course not. I would never tell anyone about you guys being witches."

I relaxed. "Thank you."

"Going back to our prior conversation, now that I know literally every witch in your life is on the same page as me, it makes me think even more that you should tell him."

"But…" I floundered for words. "What if I lose him?"

"If you don't do anything, you're going to lose him anyway." Heather held my hand. "And when has fear ever gotten in the way of your doing what needs to be done?"

All the air went out of me. I somehow managed to be brave when facing down a killer. But I couldn't have an honest conversation with the man I loved. "You're right. I just don't know if I'm strong enough to take that leap on my own."

Heather pulled out her phone and typed into it then turned it around for me to see before hitting Send.

> **HEATHER:**
> Could you come by the Izzy Bean at closing time? Dani needs to get something off her chest.

My heart clenched when the message changed to Read. A few seconds later, dots appeared as Chris typed out a response. The seconds dragged by, the dots appearing and disappearing on her screen. We stared at it together. I gripped Heather's hand. I didn't know what was worse, his agreeing to meet me or not. Agreement meant I had to go through with it. His saying no meant I had lost him already. Hope sometimes stung more than despair. At least despair would eventually lead to healing, but hope… Hope had a bad habit of just leading to more hope. Hope might require more strength than I had.

> **CHRIS:**
> OK.

I exhaled and collapsed onto the bed, and my whole body shook. The single-word response sent my brain into overdrive. *Is he excited about it? Apprehensive? What should I say?*

Heather grabbed my hands and knelt in front of me. "You've got this. You're the strongest woman I know. He would be crazy not to accept this about you. Because look at all the good you've done with your powers. You could have done a lot of bad stuff, but instead, you help families find closure. He should respect that. And if he doesn't, he isn't worthy of you. You got me?"

I nodded, my eyes still wide. Her words helped calm my nerves, and my heartbeat slowed. The weight in my chest eased up. It was still heavy, but it was bearable.

"Now, let's go get you cleaned up for your date." Heather stood and dusted off her pants.

"What about all this stuff?" I asked, glancing down at the tarp and candles.

Heather waved me off. "I'll clear it away later tonight. The cleanup company isn't due here until tomorrow."

I followed Heather back to her apartment and got ready. I had concealer in my purse that helped smooth my complexion, which had become blotchy from crying. And five minutes before the Bizzy Bean was scheduled to close, I walked downstairs. Heather relieved Becca for the night and set about cleaning up while I waited.

The closing time came and went, but Heather left the door unlocked. I tried not to stare at it, though it was hard not to. *Has he changed his mind?* I'd just stood to leave when the door opened and Chris stepped inside, wearing his deputy uniform. He wiped his feet on the mat. His hair and shirt were wet from the rain. Our eyes met, and my heart fluttered. For a second, there was warmth in his gaze, but then his eyes shuttered, and his gaze became cold and impersonal. He walked stiffly over to the table and sat down.

"Hi," I said.

He nodded.

Heather appeared at his elbow and dropped off a coffee for him and a glass of water for me. She slid a container of cornstarch across the table at me. Chris raised an eyebrow but said nothing as Heather walked away.

"Thank you for coming." I fought the urge to fidget in my seat.

Chris cleared his throat. "What did you want?"

"I..." I had been rehearsing the conversation in my head for the last hour, and I still wasn't sure if I had chosen the right direction. "I want you to know me."

"I do know you," he said.

"No, you don't."

"Then enlighten me." He searched my face. "What am I missing?"

"I have a secret. A big one. You have to promise not to freak out, okay?"

"Okay."

"Promise me," I said.

"I promise."

I reached across the table, grabbed a stir stick, and broke it in two. My mouth went dry as I reached for the cornstarch. Demonstrating my magic to Heather had worked. *What if it doesn't work this time?* I poured a bit of cornstarch onto the plate and mixed it up with water.

"What are you doing?"

"Just watch," I said.

He sighed and leaned back, his arms crossed.

My hands shook as I held the two ends of the stir stick together and smeared the cornstarch mixture along the break. I'd reread the spell at least thirty times upstairs, but it still felt awkward in my throat as I spoke the nonsensical words. His brow furrowed. He couldn't see the motes of light swirling out of my mouth and settling into the mixture. He couldn't see it flash. But he could see the cornstarch vanish.

He pushed his seat back, his eyes wide. "What the—"

"I'm a witch," I blurted.

"A witch?" He shook his head and chuckled. "That's some magic trick."

"It isn't a trick." I handed him the stick. "I'm a witch."

He scoffed and stood. "If you invited me here to play games—"

I surged to my feet. "Part of my powers are visions. Usually of people dying."

He faltered, his expression shifting from disbelief to realization to horror. "Is that how… Is that how you always seem to know things?"

"Yes," I croaked.

He took another step back, his head cocked to the side. His eyes misted as his mouth opened and closed.

I swallowed. *He's staring at me like he's never seen me before.* "This was a mistake." I bolted.

"Dani—" Chris's voice was cut off by the front door of the Bizzy Bean slamming shut behind me. Rain pelted my skin, drenching my hair and soaking my clothes in an instant.

I ran to my car with someone else's footsteps close behind me. My hands shook as I unlocked my door.

Heather grabbed me by my shoulder and yanked me around. "What happened?"

"He didn't want me." My eyes filled with tears and merged with the rainwater flowing down my face.

"What did he say?"

"Nothing!" I wailed.

"Oh, Dani." She pulled me into a hug. "He probably just needs time. It's a shock."

"You didn't," I sobbed.

Heather stroked my hair as the rain continued to fall around us. "I did. I was just better at hiding it. I channeled all my shock into excitement because that's what we both needed. This is different. Chris loves you. He told me once he thought of you as his soul mate."

"What if he's changed his mind?" I pulled back and held her gaze.

"He hasn't," she said. "He won't. Let me talk to him. I've been through the shock of this, remember?"

"Thank you." I wiped my eyes, though it was useless because of the weather. I barked out a nervous laugh. "I must look terrible."

She smiled and pulled me back into a hug. "Only a little bit."

"That's not nice." I playfully swatted at her then glanced behind her. Chris hadn't come out. He was waiting for either her or for me to come back. I had been as brave as I could muster for the day. I stepped back and gestured to the café. "You should get back in there."

She nodded and turned then trudged back to the café with her shoulders hunched against the rain. After the door closed behind her, I climbed into my car, collapsed into my seat with my head tilted back, and closed my eyes. I had badly bungled everything that day. Chris. The Retirees. *Will anyone still want to be my friend when this is all over?* I tried to connect with Charlie back at the house for comfort, but even he was annoyed with me. *Maybe I should just go home. Why do I need to be the one to fix things? I should give up investi—*

I winced as the pressure in my head spiked. Even now, with my life crumbling around me, my Sight wouldn't let me stop trying to solve the case. The mere thought of giving up made my head pound. I reached for the maps in my glove compartment. Dread over my relationship status would have to wait. I had a murder to look into. I chewed on my lip as I studied the maps. *Maybe when the case is done, I can salvage my relationships.*

Maybe... Maybe I am like my mom.

Is that why she left?

I shook my head and focused on the task at hand. The

next item on my list was tracking down Brian outside of work. He was hiding something. I could feel it.

CHAPTER 14

Focusing on the tracking spell to find Brian's car was easier said than done. My confession to Chris had been a disaster, and every other word, I lost concentration. On my sixth attempt, I finally got the words out, and the motes of light landed on Point Pleasant. My target was in town. The excitement from that revelation made the second tracking spell easier. Not only was Brian in town, but he also wasn't far. He was parked at the Unitarian Universalist church seven blocks away.

When I arrived, there were twelve vehicles in the parking lot. That was a lot of cars for a Thursday. *Maybe there's some sort of community event going on.* I craned my neck to look at the signs. Nothing was advertised. The building was mostly nondescript, a white single-story wooden structure that looked more like a community center than a church. If it weren't for the sign at the front of the parking lot, I wouldn't have been able to tell.

It was still raining. I zipped up my jacket all the way and darted out of my car to the side door, where the lights were still on. It wasn't locked, so I let myself in and followed the sound of voices to a meeting room. I cracked the door and peered inside. Fourteen people sat in a circle. The speaker, a graying middle-aged man wearing a turtleneck, looked at me as I poked my head in. He motioned me inside and smiled warmly. I couldn't back out without looking awkward, so I stepped into the room.

"Thank you, Margaret, for sharing," the man said. "Now, who would like to go next?"

Brian stood. He glared at me as he straightened, his head held high. "My name's Brian, and I'm an alcoholic."

My stomach dropped out. *I shouldn't be here.* I turned back to the door, my palms sweaty.

"I almost lost my four-month chip this week when I found out my niece had died." The anger in his voice subsided and was replaced with grief. "I'm sure some of you remember her. She was here with me that first night, when I got my day-one chip."

The group murmured. The woman sitting next to Brian reached up and squeezed his arm.

I turned back to look at Brian. He wasn't looking at me anymore. Instead, he was staring down at something in his hands. It was too small to make out, but it was small and round like an AA chip. I stood there, staring at him, as he continued.

"Before my brother died, I promised him I would take care of his daughter. His death wrecked me, though. And I gave in to all of my worst impulses. I messed everything up and in the process made it so I couldn't keep my promise to him. I was arrested for doing some really dumb stuff." He closed his eyes and swayed in place.

The entire room was silent as the group held its collective breath for him to continue. I slipped into a seat at the back of the room, my gaze transfixed.

Brian opened his eyes and shook his head. He focused on the coin in his hand again. "The first week was rough. At the end of it, my sister-in-law came to visit, and she told me I had to get my stuff together if I ever wanted to see my niece again. For eight years, I was clean and sober. For eight years, I did everything right and got out early on good behavior. Then, my first night out, I got wasted and had to start over. I've been clawing my way back to sobriety."

Everyone's eyes were on him. It was hard to look away. The emotions on his face were so raw. I inched forward in my seat. A pain formed in the back of my throat. I wasn't touching anything of his, but just being in the room with so much pain seemed to activate something in me. His emotions flowed into me, making it hard to sit there.

"I promised my brother I would look out for her. But for the past four months, she's been the one looking out for me. She was here on my first night. She stood by me when I reached my first month. I was looking forward to her being with me when I hit six months or a year. And now, all I can do is feel like I've failed her. I was supposed to be the strong one. I was the one who was supposed to take care of her. And now, she's dead, and I never got the chance—no, I had the chance. I never stepped up to do what I was supposed to do."

I clutched the edge of the seat between my knees and leaned forward. His eyes flicked to me, and his mood shifted again.

"I failed her. But I'm not going to do that again." Brian held up the chip. "I'm dedicating my chips to her. Every single one I earn for the rest of my life. I'm going to do my best to be the man she thought I was. Thank you."

I exhaled as he sat down. The rising energy in the room faded, and I slumped into my seat. The man in the turtleneck stood back up. "Thank you for sharing, Brian. I want you to know that I'm proud of you, and my heart goes out to you for your loss. I think I can speak for everyone here when I say that your niece was a bright light in this world, and it is a loss to us all that she is no longer with us. Now, does anyone else want to share?"

I slipped off my seat and inched my way toward the door as another man stood up. He introduced himself as Michael. I escaped into the hallway and padded toward the front door. I didn't get far before the door opened behind me, and Brian stormed out after me.

"Are you following me?" he asked in an angry whisper.

I glanced between him and the closed door. "I didn't mean to intrude on the meeting."

He stalked toward me and loomed. "That's not what I asked."

I took a faltering step back and put my hands out to my sides. "Sorry. I was trying to help."

"Help? Help who?" He inched forward, the vein in his forehead bulging.

"I've helped solve a few murders. I knew Linda. It was so close to home. I… I wanted to get my friend answers."

He snorted and stepped back. "Get out of here. And don't you dare come back."

I scurried away from him and sprinted to my car, where I collapsed into the front seat, my hands shaking. Brian Cartwright was a temperamental man. But the rawness of his emotions— the absolute despair over the loss of Linda and the guilt I had felt at the worksite—made sense now. It wasn't over hurting her. It was over not being there to keep her safe. Brian wasn't the killer.

CHAPTER 15

I drove home in a daze. My list of suspects was shrinking rapidly. While the boyfriend, Josh, was a piece of work, Linda's ghost had cleared him. She had just FaceTimed him before the murder, and he was nowhere near her. Mason had been getting ready for an outing with Stacey, and she seemed way too nosey not to notice him slipping away to murder someone. Brian didn't feel right. I knew in my gut it wasn't him. Which left Devin. He was still a question mark in my mind. He had been cagey about answering any questions. *Maybe Izzy has made progress.*

I pursed my lips. She was also an enigma at the moment. I had worked with her on two cases and now a third. *Is it a coincidence, or is she a medium like the Retirees suspect?* I hoped she would be home so I could ask about it gently.

My heart skipped a beat as I pulled into my driveway. It was still raining, so despite the lights being on, it was hard to see. Grace's car had been joined by a second vehicle—Chris's. I parked on the grass and checked my reflection in the rearview mirror. All the concealer I had put on had washed off in either the rain or my tears. I quickly ran my hands through my hair to smooth it down and got out of my car.

Chris's car door opened, and instead of Chris climbing out, Bob emerged. My mind whirled. I was so used to seeing Chris's sheriff vehicle that it hadn't occurred to me it would be someone else's. But the entire department drove the same make and model.

I spun away from him and stalked up my driveway to my house. "I've had an awful night. Can whatever this is wait until later?"

Bob rounded the corner of his car and grabbed my arm, yanked me around, and slammed me face first into the hood of his car. My vision swam as he pulled my arms behind my back. "Dani Williams, you are under arrest—"

"What are you doing?" I screeched.

The front door of my house opened, and Grace stepped onto the porch. She fumbled with her phone and pointed it straight at me, recording.

"For interfering with a police investigation. You have the right to remain silent. Anything you say can and will be used against you in a court of law. You have the right to an attorney. If you cannot afford an attorney, one will be provided for you. If you decide to answer questions now without an attorney present, you will still have the right to stop answering at any until you talk to an attorney. Do you understand your rights?"

"Call Heather!" I shouted at Grace.

"Do you understand your rights?" Bob repeated.

I nodded, and he yanked me back onto my feet and dragged me to the back door of his cruiser.

"Call Heather!" I shouted again.

Grace kept her phone pointed at me until Bob slammed the door shut in my face. She then backed up and closed the door. The last thing I saw before it shut was her raising her phone to her ear. I hoped that meant help was on the way.

The next half hour passed in a blur. Bob drove in silence. Once we got to the station, he had calmed down enough that he wasn't as rough as he escorted me inside. The rain poured down as we trudged up the front walkway ramp into the dilapidated double-wide they were using *temporarily* as their headquarters. I was soaked as he marched me past Peggy's desk. She stared at me wide-eyed from behind her red-framed cat-eye glasses. She hadn't liked me since the Jessica investigation, but it looked like this step took her by surprise. I had always gotten the impression she viewed me as a nuisance, and arresting nuisances wasn't normal in Point Pleasant.

The back bedroom had been converted into two holding cells. He held the door open to the empty one and motioned me forward. I didn't object and stepped inside. He undid my handcuffs, slammed the door shut behind me, and locked it. As I rubbed my wrists, I watched him stalk out of the room.

I turned slowly in place, taking in my surroundings. It was a small room with metal bars bisecting the space. The two holding cells were nearly identical. Each contained a bench-style cot. A fluorescent bulb hung in the center of the room. The window behind me had bars on it as well. I sank onto my cot and pulled my legs up to hug my knees, my heart thumping in my ears. My limbs felt heavy. *What am I doing here?* I had been asking questions about murders for months. This seemed like an extreme escalation. *Was Chris really running that much interference?*

I closed my eyes. *Maybe I should stop.* Pain spiked in the back of my head. It seemed like my Sight was hell-bent on ruining my life. *Is this the curse at work?* Dealing with my newfound powers had been mostly smooth sailing. It had been more difficult for my daughter than for me. But that was because until now, I had always followed what my Sight demanded. I stood at a crossroads: continue the investigation and possibly wreck my life or stop and maybe die from the pain. It was an impossible choice. I was damned if I did and damned if I didn't. More damned if I didn't, if I was being honest with myself.

Sighing, I dropped my legs and sat up. *If I'm stuck here and can't stop investigating, I might as well do something useful.* I muttered the words to the spell to heighten my senses. The cot under me was unbearably hard. The humming from the fluorescent lights mixed with the not-so-gentle snoring of my neighbor in the other holding cell made me sway in place. I quickly shut down the senses I didn't need and focused on the hearing.

"Are you sure about this?" Peggy's voice cut through the hum of the electronics.

"I warned her to stop. After what the guests at the bed-and-breakfast said, that she was asking questions, I couldn't ignore it. It's like the scared-straight program for kids. If we don't do something, she'll never learn, and she'll keep sticking her nose where it doesn't belong," Bob said.

Is he really treating me like a child? I sighed and shifted. The cot under me creaked loudly. I froze, trying to stop the noise so I could refocus on the conversation.

"Have they found Linda's bag yet?" Bob asked.

"No." Peggy's heels clicked against the laminate flooring. "We heard back from the phone company. The last tower it pinged from was near the bed-and-breakfast. It looks like whoever stole it removed the battery."

"What time did it get turned off?" Bob's voice was muffled by the sound of my neighbor coughing and turning over.

"At 10:57 a.m."

"So right around the time of death." Bob sighed. "I hope we get a break in the case soon."

"Me too. Have you thought about asking Da—"

"No." Bob sighed again. "Sorry. It's been a long week. Thank you for staying late, Pegs. You can head home if you need to. I'll finish up the paperwork here."

Was Peggy suggesting he talk to me? They really must not have any leads if she's considering that.

They had a long goodbye conversation about pastries and making sure her headlights were on because of the rain before she finally left. I listened for a while to the clicking of keys as Bob typed in the other room. After a while, the drain of keeping up the heightened-senses spell wore on me. I dropped it before it completely depleted my reserves and drifted off to sleep curled up on my side. The cot was hard and uncomfortable under me, but by that point, I could have slept anywhere.

I awoke to the sound of raised voices and scrambled to my feet to dart over to the bars to listen. My neighbor in the adjoining cell was doing the same. I vaguely recognized them as someone who I had seen around town. The scent of booze still rolled off them, and they swayed in place as they listened in.

"You should be ashamed of yourself, Bob." Betty's voice carried the loudest. Even from here, I could hear her stomping her foot.

"We all saw the video." Sarah's voice was pitched higher than usual. "You were unnecessarily rough, and you know it."

"You need to let her out now," Agnes added.

"Dani was interfering with a police investigation. She was warned," Bob said.

"And how exactly did she interfere, Bob?" Heather piped up next. "It's not like she was hiding any evidence. All she did was ask questions."

"I'll let her out in the morning." Bob sighed. "Now, if you ladies will—"

"No. Now. Or shall I call my father?" Olivia asked.

How many people are out there? I leaned against the bars,

straining to hear the rest. Footsteps stomped down the hall, and the door to the room flew open. Bob stalked toward me. I scrambled back from the bars as he grabbed the padlock to unlock it.

"You're free to go," he grunted.

I scampered past him and fled down the hallway. Standing in a cluster in the living-room- turned-waiting-area were the Retirees, Heather, Olivia, Willow, and Abby. Almost every single one of my friends had turned up to fight for me. Tears of gratitude welled in my eyes as they collectively pulled me into a hug then shuffled me outside.

"Are you okay?" Olivia studied my face.

I nodded. The entire interaction with Bob had been more startling than painful. "Thank you all for coming."

"I just can't stand how much of a bully he was tonight. I have half a mind to call my dad anyway," Olivia fumed. "There have to be some perks to being the mayor's daughter."

"No, it's okay." I wiped the tears from my eyes. "Honestly, I just want to get home to sleep."

They took turns giving me a hug again before wandering off to their cars.

"If he harasses you again, you promise to call us right away, okay?" Agnes asked as she clung to me.

"I promise."

The last of the group got into their vehicles, leaving me alone with Heather.

"You need a ride?" she asked.

"Yeah." I followed her to her car. "Thank you for rallying the troops."

Once we were inside, she reached over and squeezed my hand. "You know we'll always try to help you when we can."

"That's good to know." I smiled sheepishly. "I'm going to need it."

Heather raised an eyebrow.

"I got another lead to look into."

She barked out a laugh. "You're still investigating after all this?"

I stared out the window as we drove away from the sheriff's station. "Of course. I have to."

We drove home in companionable silence. I leaned my head against the glass. It was easy to say yes when I didn't really have a choice. But from everything I had learned about Linda over the last few days, she seemed worth it.

CHAPTER 16

Something woke me, but my brain was too foggy from sleep for me to focus on anything. I lay there, my eyes still closed, as my mind fought against my body to stay awake. A light was on somewhere. *Is that green?* I groaned as the noise that had woken me sounded again. It was Charlie growling.

I rolled over in bed. With my eyes open, I could tell the light was coming from the hallway. It was one of those warm LED lights we had put in around the house. Grace was standing in the doorway, silhouetted by the hall light. I squinted at her as Charlie continued to growl next to me.

"What are you doing?" I asked.

Grace flinched. "Sorry. I didn't mean to wake you. I wanted to make sure you made it home all right. I was worried."

Sleep was pulling at my mind, so it was hard to focus. *Her words are fine. But her voice? What's wrong with it?* It took a moment for the strangeness to settle in. Her voice had been oddly flat, without her usual cadence or warmth.

"I'm fine." I yawned and wiped at my face, struggling to keep my eyes open.

Charlie growled again. It came from deep in his chest. I

could feel his unrest through our bond. As my mind connected to his, the hair on the back of my neck raised. My heartbeat quickened, and I subconsciously held my breath. I let it out shakily. *What on earth?* I pushed myself up to a sitting position. My muscles were weak, and my whole body felt heavy.

Grace was still standing in the doorway, staring at me.

I swallowed, my mouth suddenly dry. "Is something wrong, sweetheart?"

"No. I love you, Mom." Grace stepped back into the hallway and closed the door behind her.

Charlie settled down and curled into a ball. His eyes were trained on the doorway, his tail twitching as he stared. I slipped out of bed, tiptoed to the door, and peeked out into the hall. It was empty. I stepped out. As I rested my hand on the doorknob, my jaw clenched, and my whole body tensed. Heat rushed through me, and my stomach fluttered. I stumbled back into my room. The emotions radiating off the door were a strange mix of hatred and confusion. *What the—?*

Quickly, I pushed the door closed and locked it. My heart raced. *Was that my daughter or someone pretending to be her?* I hadn't received the test results back from Megan yet. If Grace were possessed by Meredith, that could have been her. I grabbed the chair from the corner and pushed it up against the door.

Then I backed away until my legs hit the bed. I collapsed onto it, pulling my legs up after me. My heart was still beating a mile a minute. I stared wide-eyed at the door as I hugged my legs to my chest.

After twenty minutes, the initial terror abated, and I crawled under the covers. But I was still too wired to sleep. I lay there, staring at the door and petting Charlie. My eyelids grew heavier by the minute.

Almost an hour later, the door handle jiggled. I sat bolt upright and stared at it.

Is she...? I pulled my legs to my chest again. My daughter —or someone pretending to be her—had just tried to come into my room again. I never thought I would be scared to be home alone with my family. Then I remembered I wasn't home alone, and a chill ran through my body. Izzy was in the guest room in the daylight basement. I scrambled over to my nightstand and grabbed my phone. Without thinking, I dialed her number.

Izzy answered on the third ring. She sounded like she was talking to me from inside a tunnel, the sound of cars in the background. "Is everything all right?" she asked.

"Yeah, I just... Where are you?"

"I couldn't sleep. I thought a drive might help." Izzy sighed. "I probably went too far, though. I'm in Issaquah. You think they'll have an all-night diner? I could really go for some waffles. And like a gallon of coffee."

I collapsed against my headboard. Izzy wasn't home. She was safe. "Do you think coffee is wise?"

"Probably not."

"Be safe out there."

"Don't worry. I will. See you in the morning," Izzy said and hung up.

I couldn't get back to sleep after that. So I grabbed the newest notebook I'd received from Megan and tried to read through it. But I couldn't focus on the words. I kept staring at the door, wondering when the knob was going to move again. I lay like that until the sun rose.

Under the light of day, the chair in the front of the door began to look ridiculous. *I don't know what she was thinking about when she came in. What if she was thinking about Bob? Of course she would hate him. He just arrested me.* I slid under my covers and stared up at the ceiling. *It could have been anything. Am I reading too much into it?*

Before I knew it, I had fallen back asleep.

After my late-night ordeal, I ended up sleeping in. By the time I arrived at the Bizzy Bean, the morning rush had passed, and there were only a few stragglers left behind, typing away at their laptops as kittens scampered around underfoot. Heather was standing behind the counter, chatting with Becca. I waved, and she excused herself to join me.

"Finally," she said as she slid in across from me at our usual booth. "I've been waiting for hours for an update."

I ducked my head. I hadn't been up to giving the update the previous night. Too much had happened. But after I'd caught up on some much-needed sleep, my thoughts were clearer. Devin was the only one left on my list, but I couldn't help but feel I was missing something. I filled her in on my investigation. She agreed Brian should be taken off the list of suspects.

"Anyway, it sounds like the sheriff is still looking for her bag. Had you heard it was missing?" I asked.

Heather froze. "They asked me if she brought one into work with her that day. I'm sorry. I didn't think about it at all. You think the killer took it?"

"Took what?" Izzy asked as she appeared next to our table.

I scooted over to let her in. "I heard last night that Linda's bag is missing. The sheriff is still looking for it."

Izzy winced when I said the word *sheriff*. "Grace mentioned what happened last night when I got back this morning. Are you doing okay?"

"I'm fine." I studied Izzy. Her eyes were still bloodshot from lack of sleep. "How about you? You look exhausted."

Izzy shrugged. "It has to be something about sleeping in old houses. I mean, don't get me wrong. I am totally appreciative that you are letting me stay at your place. But I'm looking forward to moving back into my own apartment this afternoon. All the creaking. And Grace staying up talking half the night. I've barely slept."

"Did you sleep at all last night?"

She shook her head. "Drove half the night. I stopped at Snoqualmie Pass and watched the sun rise. I thought when I got back, I would be tired enough to sleep. But all those little noises just kept me up."

I glanced down. Her elbow was touching the back of our seat. I slid my hand behind me and touched the bench rest. Exhaustion rolled through me, and I tried not to yawn. "I've never noticed. Honestly, it almost sounds like you're haunted."

Amusement flowed through the wood into my hand as Izzy giggled.

"If ghosts were real, maybe." She shook her head. "Haunted? Could you imagine?"

There was no deception in her response. She was amused by the idea. *The Retirees said a medium would know they're one, since they're born with the power. I guess she isn't one, then. But why was Linda so convinced Izzy was ignoring her? What has she been trying to communicate? She said someone was a liar. Devin?* He was the last name on my suspect list.

"Yeah, not sure what I was thinking," I said. "Have you had any luck getting Devin to open up to you?"

Izzy deflated. "Not well. He's just as tight-lipped now as when I began. All he wants to do is talk about my work. It's like he's never heard of an arts-and-entertainment reporter before."

I sighed and slumped into the booth. My eyes bounced from face to face around the room until my gaze slid past them all to the sidewalk. Standing across the street, in his usual spot, was the young man with the clipboard, collecting signatures for a cause. He had been around town all week for something, but I hadn't stopped to talk to him yet.

A smile broke across my face as I stared at him. He would

have had a clear view of the building in the days leading up to the murder. He might have seen something. "Have either of you talked to him?" I pointed out the window.

Heather and Izzy turned to follow my gaze.

Heather shook her head.

"I don't think so," Izzy admitted.

"I think I'm going to go talk to him," I said.

Izzy slid out of the booth to let me up. She yawned and wiped at her eyes.

"Why don't I get you a double shot of expresso while Dani does her thing?" Heather suggested.

"That would be wonderful." Izzy followed Heather to the counter as I strode past them to the door.

I made a beeline for the young gentleman. He was dressed in cargo pants and a blue T-shirt with a puffy green jacket over the top, and he held his clipboard out in front of him.

He smiled at me as I approached. "Good morning, ma'am. Do you know much about orcas?"

I returned his smile. "I'm sorry. No. But I actually wanted to talk to you about something else if you have a few minutes."

"All right." He dropped the clipboard to his side. "How can I be of assistance?"

I pulled out my phone and opened Linda's social media profile. I showed him a photo of her. "Do you recognize this woman?"

"Yeah. Linda's great. I haven't seen her in a few days, though. Is she okay?"

My heart sank. *He doesn't know.* I smiled at him sympathetically and stepped closer. I softened the tone of my voice. "I'm sorry to be the one to tell you this, but she died."

"Oh gosh." His eyes widened, and he covered his mouth. "What happened?"

"Someone… She was murdered. Across the street. It was a few days ago."

He dropped his hand, his brow furrowing. "Is that why the sheriff's office was swarming the building?"

I nodded. "I'm helping, trying to give the family some closure. Do you remember if she had any problems with anyone?"

He shook his head. "No. She was so friendly, got along with everyone just fine. She was the only one who stopped to say hi to me every day. And she did that with everyone. I saw her make time for each of the guests in that place."

"Oh?"

"Yeah. She took Stacey her coffee every morning. It wasn't part of the service, but she liked to go the extra mile. And she even helped that artist by carrying his supplies in."

My mind went blank. *Artist?* "Who?"

"I think he said his name was Devin." He lowered his voice. "I probably shouldn't be telling you this, since it's a secret. But he's the street artist the mayor hired to do all the murals."

Did Linda find out? Or did she already know? That's an odd thing to kill over.

"I can't believe she's gone," he said.

"Did you see Devin the day the sheriff's office was here?"

"Yeah, he left mid-morning. Why?"

My chest expanded. I felt light as energy coursed through me. "Do you remember what time he left?"

"Around nine thirty."

"What time did he get back?"

"I'm not sure." He gave me a quizzical look. "He was still gone when I left for lunch at one."

My heart sank. If he was gone from nine thirty to one, he couldn't have done it. Linda was murdered around eleven o'clock. "Are you sure about those times?"

"Yes, ma'am."

"Have you seen her talking to anyone else?" I asked.

"Sure, every customer. She was nice to everyone. I even saw her helping that real estate developer a few times."

I cocked my head to the side. *But Mason said he didn't know Linda.* "Would you be able to describe him to me?"

"Average height. Nicely dressed. Black hair, with a distinct widow's peak." He held his hand up in a sharp V.

"Thank you," I said.

"They got coffee together a few times. She was really excited that last time I saw her. A trust account her dad had left her had just opened up, and she was planning on using it to buy her and her uncle a house. Mason was going to help her." He looked between me and the coffee shop, his blue eyes misting. "She said she wanted to do something good with it. Do you think he did something to her to get that money?"

"I don't know." I patted his shoulder. "Thank you so much for telling me what you knew. You should probably give a statement to the police, too, just in case they have any follow-up questions."

He nodded and swallowed. "I had no idea. I thought she was busy with classes, you know?"

I expressed my condolences and walked back to the café. As I went, I replayed my conversation with Mason in my head. He had claimed not to know her, but when I asked about whether they saw anything, Mason wasn't the one who responded. It was Stacey. She was the one who said no. She was the one who claimed they were both getting ready for a stroll. But if they had separate rooms, there was no way for her to know for sure he was in his own. I had assumed an alibi from the beginning, so I hadn't looked any closer. Mason was the *liar*.

CHAPTER 17

By the time I reached the door to the Bizzy Bean, I was almost at a full run. I burst through the doors and stumbled as I slid to a stop in front of the counter.

Heather gaped at me. "What on earth—?"

"It was Mason."

Her face went as white as a sheet. "Mason? Are you sure?"

"Ninety-nine-point-nine-nine percent?"

She grimaced. "He checked out right before you got here."

I cursed under my breath and grabbed my cell phone. He had a head start, but I had to find him. When I pulled up his website, his robust real estate portfolio had been replaced with a page saying Site under Construction. All the photos of his business were gone.

I hung my head and closed my eyes. *Focus, Dani. If you can't find him, then what can you find?* My eyes snapped open, and I searched for Linda instead. Bob had mentioned her bag was missing. I was willing to bet Mason had taken it. I flipped through photos until I found one with a clear view of the bag she wore in most of them. Turning the phone around, I showed it to Heather. "Was Linda carrying this bag when she came in that day?"

Heather nodded. "She almost always had it on her. Said it was the only purse big enough to carry her wallet and textbooks at the same time."

Izzy emerged from the bathroom and slid up next to me at the counter. "How'd it go?"

I barely looked at her as I studied the purse. "I got a new lead. Be right back."

I darted out the door.

"Where are you—" Izzy's voice was cut off by the door closing behind me.

I didn't have time to chat. Mason had a head start, and I couldn't be sure he still had the bag with him. I ran to my car and threw myself into the front seat. After yanking the maps out of the glove compartment, I flipped to the page that had Point Pleasant on it. In one hand, I held up my phone and in the other, the map. I'd used this version of the tracking spell often enough over the last few days that I didn't even have to think about it. The words weren't even halfway out of my mouth when they flowed to a spot on the map. It was in the middle of a wooded area north of town.

I grabbed another atlas from my glove box. That one was of trails of the Pacific Northwest. I recast the spell, and the lights flew to a spot not too far away from a trailhead. I drew an *X* over the spot and scrambled out of my car and back to the café.

Izzy and Heather were still gathered around the counter when I stomped back inside and tossed the map down between them. "We should go there."

"What for?" Izzy glanced between me and the map.

Shoot. I hadn't stopped to think of an explanation. I was just going on pure instinct. "Mason lied about knowing Linda. I think he took her bag when he killed her, and her cell phone last pinged at that location. I suspect he stashed it there. And since he's checked out of his room, I'm willing to bet he's on his way there now to collect it before getting out of town."

"Okay. Becca, do you mind watching the café for a bit?" Heather asked.

Becca stepped out from the kitchen with a tray of cookies. She nodded as she put them into the display case. "Sure thing."

Heather grabbed her coat, lifted the flip-up countertop, and let herself out.

Izzy scrambled back to our table to get her coat then followed us out to my car. We piled inside and drove in silence to the trailhead. The whole way, I gripped the wheel, my knuckles turning white. Heather stared straight ahead, her jaw clenched. And Izzy fidgeted in the back seat, her fingers running along the edge of her seat belt as she chewed on her lip, her pink hair hanging loose around her shoulders.

The trailhead was a twenty-minute drive from the Bizzy Bean. Winter still clung to the shadows even as the spring rains tried to warm things up. There was a single car parked in the small lot when we arrived.

Heather inhaled sharply when she saw it. "That's Mason's vehicle."

"Are you sure?" I asked.

"Positive."

We climbed out and looked around. Despite only being a mile from town, it felt deserted out there. It was amazing what a thick line of trees could do. I put my hand on the hood of his car. It was still warm. We weren't far behind him.

"We should go in after him," I said.

Izzy pulled her jacket closed around her. "Are you sure? Shouldn't we call the cops first?"

"We don't know how much longer he's going to be out here." I shivered as a cool breeze swept past me. "I don't want to lose him."

"Why don't we call them first then go in? Then we'll at least know backup is on the way," Heather suggested.

"All right." I sighed. "But then we go in."

They both nodded. Izzy pulled out her phone and dialed. I stomped my feet, trying to keep them warm. The rain from the previous day had flash frozen in places, and my foot broke through the thin layer of ice. Mud coated my boots. Gritting my teeth, I pulled out my foot, and the mud made a squelching sound as my foot came loose.

Izzy hung up with the cops, and we all exchanged looks then headed into the woods.

Under the tree canopy, it almost felt like twilight. Most of the trees were evergreens, with the occasional bare red alder thrown into the mix. The thick moss on the alder tree trunks combined with the Douglas fir trees made everything green. But it also dampened sound and helped block the weak sunlight that was peeking through the dense cloud cover. The trail wound through the trees in an almost zigzagging pattern as it climbed up a small hill.

We trudged along in silence, straining our ears to hear anything. Birds called to one another in the distance. The occasional twig snapped in the underbrush. The first time, we spun around as a group only to see a terrified opossum fall onto its side, playing dead.

After five minutes, we came to a fork in the road.

"Which way?" Heather whispered.

The trail to the right sloped downward. Ferns clustered around the edges of the path. The trail to the left was mostly level, and broken branches cluttered the walkway. I pulled out the map. It showed the path became a loop, and the two sides would eventually meet. My hand-drawn *X* was too large, so I couldn't tell which side was closer.

"Should we split up?" Izzy asked.

My mouth went dry. I swallowed, pushing down the fear.

"How about Izzy, you go left, Heather, you go right, and I'll go off trail to keep you both in sight?"

They each stared at their prospective roads.

"All right," Heather said, breaking the silence. She stepped onto her path.

Izzy followed suit to the right. My head swiveled between them as they padded away from me. I shook out my arms, trying to release the tension building in my shoulders, and took my first tentative step forward into the underbrush. Pushing down my fear, I steadied my breathing. This wasn't the first time I had chased a killer. At least this time, I had backup within shouting distance.

I continued onward. By the warmth of his car, I knew Mason was only a few minutes ahead of us. *We can catch him.*

No. We will catch him.

CHAPTER 18

I glanced back to the left. There were too many trees in the way, and I had lost sight of Izzy. When I swiveled my head to the right, Heather was nowhere to be seen as well. *I'm alone. They've left you here.* I shook my head, trying to banish the intrusive thoughts. Heather would never leave me behind. I needed to get this done so I could get back home where it was safe.

I grabbed my phone and pulled up the picture of Linda and her bag again. My signal was weak so far into the tree line, but the photo eventually loaded. I concentrated on the image of the purse and murmured the words to an alternative tracking spell I knew. The one with the maps was useful for finding things far away, but when it was nearby, it was so much simpler to follow a trail. The motes of light swirled out of my mouth and formed a line that snaked to the left. Shoving my phone back into my pocket, I followed it.

The trail came to a stop in the middle of a small clearing. Sunlight streamed through an opening in the canopy. Ferns had overtaken the ground until every inch was covered in their foliage. The trail led straight into the center of the clearing and disappeared into the leaves. I glanced around.

Izzy and Heather were still nowhere to be seen. So deep in the woods, the path had vanished.

My feet squelched in the mud as I trudged my way through the ferns. I tried to pad lightly, but with each step, my feet sank deeper into the muck, and I had to yank my foot out before taking another step. About halfway through, the ground became harder. I stepped onto a patch of solid earth inches from my quarry, knelt in front of the fern where the path of light ended, and pushed aside the leaves. Sitting there, hidden by the foliage, was Linda's missing purse.

I pulled the bag from its hiding space, but I couldn't pick up any of the emotional residue on the bag through my thick winter gloves. My hands shook as I pushed open the flap and peered inside. My mouth went dry. It was stuffed to the brim with cash.

A twig broke behind me, and the hair on the back of my neck instantly stood on end. I rolled to the side. A large branch swung through the space my head had been a millisecond before, and my vision swam as it caught the edge of my skull. I had been fast but not fast enough. I continued rolling as Mason cursed. His foot had become stuck in the mud.

I landed on solid earth. The entire field wasn't muddy, just the section I had traipsed through to get there.

Mason yanked his foot free and scrambled after me, swinging the branch back and slamming it down next to me as I rolled away a second time. When I kicked out at him, my foot connected with the branch, and it cracked in his hands. He tossed it aside and lunged toward me, his fingers grabbing me.

"It's mine! You can't have it!" he snarled as he knelt on my chest, his hands wrapped around my throat.

I clawed at him with my right hand as my lungs burned. With my left hand, I felt along the ground next to me, searching for something, anything, to use against him. My hand landed on Linda's bag. I grabbed it and swung it upward. When it landed, he snarled and clutched at the side of his head.

I kicked him between the legs, and he doubled over, staggering backward. On my hands and knees, I scrambled away from him.

"Help!" I screamed. I surged to my feet and sprinted away, into the tree line.

Someone gasped behind me. I glanced over my shoulder to see how far away he was. He hadn't moved from his position. My heart sank as my eyes landed on Izzy. He held her by her throat as she beat at him ineffectually with her fists.

"Let her go," I said.

He stared at me, his hair hanging limply over his forehead. Mud covered his shirt and pants. Some of it had splashed his face.

"I said let her go." I stepped toward him, my knees shaking. It took everything I had to continue facing him.

"Give it back," he said.

I glanced down at my hand. I was still holding Linda's bag. In my haste to get away, it hadn't registered that I was still holding it. I tossed it down.

He sneered at me. Izzy's eyes widened as his grip tightened around her neck. I mentally went through the list of spells I could remember. Tracking someone or heightening my senses wouldn't be useful. I didn't want to freak Izzy out any further, and the darkness spell would probably terrify her. *Why didn't I spend more time with the new book? There has to be something in there that's useful.* Try as I might, I couldn't remember the words to the spell that charmed a person. I wasn't even sure if it would work in the situation. His hate for me was too strong.

Hate... That's a negative emotion. During my first showdown with Marsha, I had cast a spell out of instinct. I didn't know the words. I just had the intention. And it had worked.

Megan said it was easier to manipulate a negative emotion than a positive one. The positive required more finesse. But fear, I could use. It didn't need to be a scalpel. A sledge hammer would work just fine.

I breathed in deeply, filling my lungs. I remembered everything that had scared me after the past few weeks and funneled it inside—becoming a witch; facing down killers; the thought I was losing my daughter to a dead woman's influence. Each fear piled, one after the other, onto each other, and I exhaled, pointing at him. A torrent of golden lights flew out of my mouth toward him. With every fiber of my being, I wanted him to feel afraid.

The lights slammed into him and swirled under his skin, lighting him up like a Christmas tree. He yelled, a wordless wail, and flung Izzy aside. Her head bounced off a stump half-hidden under the foliage. Instead of running away, he flung himself at me.

I flew backward, landing hard on the ground as he pummeled me with his fists. Rolling onto my back, I held up my arms to protect my head. Through my forearms, he snarled at me. A brown contact had come loose and slid down his face, revealing a green eye underneath. He was wordless in his fury, spittle forming on his lips.

"Over here!" Heather yelled.

He didn't acknowledge Heather's presence, just kept reaching for me, his hands clawing at my arms.

Then he was sailing away as Deputy Harrison Abbott yanked him off me.

I collapsed to the ground, my breathing ragged as I stared at Mason. He was snarling like a wild animal, still trying to get at me as Harrison pinned him down.

Heather stumbled into the clearing with Chris close on her heels. She ran over to Izzy and touched her forehead. Izzy winced and sat up. When Chris took a step toward me, I met his gaze. His eyes were wide, his pupils dilated. His mouth hung open in shock. He took another stumbling step toward me.

Mason wrenched himself free from Harrison's grasp and threw himself toward me, but Harrison grabbed him by the ankles and held him. Chris pivoted toward Mason and grabbed him by the shoulders to restrain him. The lights of my spell were still swirling under Mason's skin. I couldn't figure out how to drop it. I willed it to end, but Mason was fully under its thrall. Chris held Mason firmly, and he and Harrison got a pair of handcuffs on him.

I staggered to my feet and stood staring at the scene. Mason was a whimpering mess. Izzy was bleeding from a wound on her forehead. Chris and Harrison were panting from the exertion of holding Mason down. The poor ferns had been trampled. And every one of us was covered from head to foot in mud. The absurdity of the sight hit me, and I giggled uncontrollably.

Tears quickly replaced the giggles, and before I knew it, I was kneeling in the mud, crying. I was never going to get used to facing down a killer, no matter how many times I ran headlong after them.

Mason was still thrashing against Chris's hold. Chris stared at me then exchanged looks with Heather.

She nodded, scurried over to me, and wiped the mud from my face with the sleeve of her jacket. "Are you hurt?"

I shook my head. Most of his blows had landed on my forearms. They would be sore in the morning, but there was no permanent damage.

She helped me to my feet. As we all walked back to the road to my car, I leaned on her. When we were halfway down the path, the spell faded, and Mason lost his will to fight. He stumbled along in silence in front of us, Chris holding him so he wouldn't run. Harrison carried Izzy in his arms. For such a tall, skinny guy, he was surprisingly strong.

We stumbled out of the woods, and I blinked against the

brightness of the sun. Harrison gently put Izzy down on the curb. Heather and I sat next to her, waiting for an ambulance to arrive. She had a nasty gash on her forehead.

The first car to arrive was Bob's. I clenched my teeth as he stepped out of his vehicle.

"If he asks..." I leaned over to Izzy and Heather. "Please tell him I remembered Mason talking about hiking out here."

Heather nodded.

Izzy stared at me, bleary-eyed, as Bob stomped toward us.

"Please," I whispered.

"Why are these three women left sitting together?" Bob bellowed. "Don't you know anything about proper questioning protocol?"

I scrambled to my feet and stepped away from the group, holding up my hands. "It's okay. I'll go sit by my car. I was just checking on my friend."

I stalked over to my car and took a seat on the hood. I glanced at Izzy, but she looked away. *What is she going to tell him?*

"Get him down to the station." Bob pointed at Chris.

I watched, my heart fluttering, as Chris put Mason into the back seat of his car and drove away. Then I followed Bob and Harrison with my eyes as they moved from Heather to Izzy and back to Heather. They were about to talk to Izzy a second time when the ambulance arrived to take her away. They asked her a few more questions as she was loaded onto a stretcher. And only then did they turn to talk to me.

Bob marched over to me, his footfalls heavy. He leaned forward to loom over me, his hands behind his back, making his shoulders appear even wider. He stared down his nose at me. "How did you know to come here?"

"I remembered Mason talking about hiking out here. He had muddy boots the day after Linda died. I thought maybe he hid something out here. And when I found out he checked out early, it seemed like a good idea to come check this place out just in case."

"Very convenient." He grunted. "You're free to go."

I slid off the hood and grabbed a few towels from the trunk of my car. Sometimes, inspection got messy, and it was good to have something on hand to clean up with—or to use to protect my seats. I was still covered in mud, so I put the towels on the front seats and climbed into my car. Heather got in a minute later.

"Is everything going okay?" she asked.

I shrugged and drove away. "I'm sure this is just going to make Bob hate me even more."

"I'm just glad you weren't hurt." She squeezed my hand, and we traveled back into town in silence.

I had thrown a fear spell at Mason, and he had gone berserk. *Does he have a really strong fight instinct? Or did I do something wrong?* I mulled it over. There had to be something wrong with my intention with the spell. I just couldn't figure out what. The more I poked at the problem, the more confused I became. I replayed the moment I'd cast the spell over in my head. I had given him fear. *Did I give him my fight instinct? Do I have a fight instinct?* His rage had been so blind. I'd never been that angry before. It was unsettling. *Maybe there's just something wrong with him.* That felt right. He was a killer, after all.

CHAPTER 19

It had been two days since my altercation with Mason, and I ached all over—nothing strong enough to keep me out of the office but enough that I noticed it every time I moved. I glanced at the clock. It was just before six o'clock. Heather had asked me to meet her at the beach at six for our traditional case recap after a successful investigation. So I packed my bag and drove my car to the pier.

The sun was low in the sky as I climbed down the steps to the beach. A warm breeze came in off the water. It was a pleasant change and hinted at the coming spring. When I rounded a pile of rocks, I came up short. My breath caught in my throat. Twenty feet away was a picnic blanket with a small circle of candles and lanterns around it. And standing next to them, holding a basket, was Chris.

Music started playing as I walked toward him. My stomach somersaulted as I recognized the lyrics to "Truly, Madly, Deeply" by Savage Garden. I had been obsessed with their music in high school. It was the song Ed, my ex-husband, had played when he asked me out. My gaze bounced around as I closed the gap between us. Almost every aspect of the setup was the same.

"What is this?" I asked.

"You shared your secret with me." He cleared his throat. "I thought it was only fair that I share the only secret I've ever kept from you."

I swallowed. My heart was going a mile a minute, and my palms were sweaty. I didn't know if I should be excited or scared. My body was trying to be both.

"I knew you were coming up for the summer after high school graduation. I spent weeks trying to figure out how to ask you out. And I made the mistake of telling my best friend about my plans, and… well… we both know how that went. He swooped in and stole my plans, and you ended up together.."

I gaped. Ed asking me out on the beach had been his one and only grand romantic gesture for our entire relationship. It had never occurred to me he didn't know how to do them without help.

"Well, almost all my plans." Chris flipped open the lid of the picnic basket to reveal s'more donuts.

My mouth watered at the sight. They looked exactly like the donuts I used to buy at Frankie's donuts on the boardwalk, right down to the toasted marshmallow swirl on top. They'd been my favorite dessert for years and probably still would be if it weren't for the fact that Frankie's had been closed for well over a decade. "Where did you get these?"

"They are as close to the originals as I could get. I still have Frankie's number from when I used to work there. It took some doing, but he was willing to share the recipe with me. And Heather was more than willing to give making them a try."

I licked my lips, and my stomach rumbled.

Chris laughed and motioned for me to sit. His eyes were light and trusting. Apparently, the decision that had been weighing on his mind for the past few days had been made. If the donuts were any indication, he had made a wonderful decision.

I sat down across from him.

He put down the basket and plopped down across from me. "I'm still trying to wrap my head around your being a witch. I was in complete shock when you told me. At first, I didn't want to believe it, but... then Heather came back in after you ran away and talked to me about it. She asked me one question that really helped me see things clearly."

I swallowed, my mouth dry, then licked my lips, trying to wet them. "And what question was that?"

"Do you think that this makes Dani a different person?"

My hands trembled. I clasped them in my lap to hide the shaking. "Does it?"

He shook his head.

I exhaled, my shoulders relaxing.

"It doesn't change who you are. You are still the kindest woman I know and still the woman I fell in love with. And when she told me about... your visions and that you can't stop them, it all made sense. Why you investigate. Why you push so hard for answers."

"So... you're not mad at me anymore?"

"No. I realized this past week you're going to investigate anyway." He cleared his throat. "I'm going to need you to promise me something, though, if this is going to work."

My heart skipped a beat. I wanted to say I would do anything, but blind promises almost always led to heartache. "What do you need me to promise?"

"That you won't cut me out of things again. That you'll tell me everything."

I opened my mouth, but he held up his hands.

"And in return, when you tell me you need me to stand down because it's a witch thing, I will."

"Are you sure?" I asked. "I might need you to stand down

for very odd-sounding reasons sometimes. Are you really prepared for that?"

"When the alternative is losing you? Every day of the week."

I studied him. This was everything I had ever wanted—a partnership with someone who trusted me implicitly. I wasn't sure what I had done to deserve him. My heart swelled, and a smile broke out across my face. "Yes. I promise. I promise I'll tell you everything."

He sagged, relief on his face. Then he sat up on his knees and leaned across the space between us. I met him halfway. My skin tingled in anticipation. He held my gaze as he leaned in closer, his eyelids only fluttering closed at the last second as our lips touched.

It was as magical as our first kiss. Electricity coursed through my body. This was meant to be. He was who I was meant to be with. I leaned into it and kissed him back.

After a minute, he pulled away, sat back on his heels, and twisted around until he was seated next to me. He raised his arm, and I slid under it, cuddling up to his side.

"Does this mean we're back together?" I asked.

He slid a key into my hand and kissed the top of my head. "And even stronger than before."

"Is this what I think it is?" I held up the plain silver house key.

"We've been dancing around taking the next step for months. Now that we know each other's secrets, I thought it was only fair that you have a key to my place."

"Did Heather mention that I'm cursed?"

He squeezed me. "She did."

I sank into his arms, my head resting on his shoulder. "I'm going to need a drawer."

"It's already empty," he whispered as he kissed the top of my head.

My hand closed around the key as warmth coursed through me. He was still nervous. I could feel that. But he loved me, and we were going to make it work. We sat watching the sunset, eating donuts together.

"Heather is probably impatiently waiting to hear how this went," Chris said as the last of the light disappeared.

I laughed and helped him clean up. We packed everything back into the picnic basket then walked hand in hand to the Bizzy Bean.

The café had closed for the night, but the lights in the back were still on, and the front door was unlocked. I knocked on the glass as we entered. Heather came running out of the kitchen, her red hair piled in a messy bun on top of her head. When she saw us standing there holding hands, a grin spread across her face from ear to ear.

"It worked?" she asked.

"We're together." I held up our hands.

Heather bounced in place. "Finally!"

Chris and I chuckled.

I stepped away from him to pull Heather into a hug. "Thank you so much. The donuts you made were perfect."

Heather blushed and swatted my back. "It was just the icing on top of an already very romantic gesture."

We followed Heather to our usual booth in the back. Under the better light of the booth, Heather grimaced when she saw my face. She touched a bruise that had formed along my jawline. "How are you feeling?"

I winced. "I've seen better days. But honestly, I'm more worried about Izzy. She came and got her stuff yesterday while I was at work. I haven't seen her yet to see how she's holding up. She texted to say she was okay. But… she looked rough, you know?"

"You never explained how you figured out it was Mason who did it," Heather said.

"Remember when we first talked to him about Linda? He claimed he didn't know her?"

Heather nodded.

"When I was talking to the guy with the clipboard—"

"Logan," Heather interjected.

"When I spoke to Logan, he mentioned he saw Linda and Mason talking a few times. He said that Linda had just come into some money when a trust opened up and was planning on buying a house with Mason's help. I thought, 'Why would he lie about that?' And the only explanation I could come up with was because he did it. He killed her."

"He made a full confession yesterday," Chris said.

"Did he say why he did it?" Heather asked.

"He's a con man." Chris paused for dramatic effect. "He was running a fake real estate investor scheme on older women. He thought Stacey was an easy mark, and through her, he could get access to her late husband's estate. Her husband left her millions. He hadn't planned on targeting Linda at all, but his greed got the better of him. She was very trusting and gave him a lot of her money. What he wasn't counting on was her finding his fake IDs while cleaning his room. When she found them, she realized what he was and confronted him to get her money back. He panicked and killed her."

"Did he say why he moved the body to Izzy's room?" I asked.

"It had been empty all week, and he didn't know a guest was checking in that day. He thought he would have time to move her after dark," Chris said.

Heather got up to get us all hot chocolates. When she came back, the conversation shifted to happier topics. We chatted for a few more hours, until we were all yawning and ready for bed. I wished Heather farewell and left the Bizzy Bean the way I had come in: hand in hand with Chris.

He walked me back to my car. Once we reached it, he

lingered, staring into my eyes. "Thank you for telling me the truth."

"Thank you for being able to handle the truth." I stood on my tiptoes and kissed him good night, then he watched me as I climbed into my car and drove away.

I smiled the whole way home. It really had been the perfect night.

CHAPTER 20

My heart was still light when I pulled up in front of my house. I stared in puzzlement at the car in my driveway. It didn't belong to Grace, but it was vaguely familiar. I climbed out of my car and walked toward the front door. A shape moved on the porch, and I faltered as it took shape, then Megan stepped out of the shadows.

"Oh gosh, I hope you haven't been sitting out here for long. What are you doing out here so late?" I asked.

"I would have called, but we keep forgetting to exchange numbers." Megan smiled weakly. "I want you to know that even though we just met, I have really been enjoying feeling like we could be friends."

I cocked my head. *Could be?* "We can."

"I hope so. I really hope you still want to be after you hear what I've come to say."

A chill crept down my spine. She had such sadness in her eyes. "Why are you here?" I whispered.

"I am so sorry. I had no choice." Megan's voice broke.

"What—"

"The Wardens are coming." Tears flowed down her face. "After the curse, after how it twisted my family, they've had us under a compulsion to contact them if we find out certain things are happening. And those things are happening. I am so sorry. The Wardens are going to have questions for every member of your coven."

My mind whirled with questions. I couldn't get them out fast enough. "My coven? What coven? The Retirees? Why?"

"Don't run. They'll assume you're guilty. Just answer their questions, and everything... Everything will be all right."

I scurried up the stairs toward her and grabbed her arms. Holding her gaze, I willed her to give me an explanation. "What's going on? Please, just tell me what happened."

"I finished looking at the sample you gave me," she sobbed.

My stomach dropped. I gaped at her. *This is about Grace?*

"She isn't being charmed. She isn't possessed. At least not by Meredith. She's under the influence of something far worse."

I opened and closed my mouth. *What could be worse than the witch who cursed us?*

"She's under the influence of an Outsider. The same Outsider that twisted Meredith's mind."

An Outsider? Aren't they mentioned in the third law of magic? Do not augment our power through deals with Outsiders? "What is an Outsider?" I stammered.

Megan sagged and leaned against the wooden railing. "They're hard to explain. They're beings that live beyond our reality. Outside our reality. It's why they're called Outsiders. They go by many names, but most commonly, they're referred to as the Fae."

I stumbled back. *Fairies are real?* Images of cute nymphs danced through my head. But the look on her face said they were much darker. My thoughts turned to the Brothers Grimm and every evil fairy tale I had ever heard. *Grace is involved with the Fae?*

"This Outsider is already making Grace do things."

"We already knew that. She's been going to Meredith's—"

"Not just at Meredith's house." Megan shook her head and reached out to hold my hand. "I felt it the second I walked onto your property. Don't you feel it?"

"Feel what?"

"How your emotions are heightened here? How hard it is to focus?"

I swallowed. My mouth was bone dry. The hairs on my arms and neck were standing up. The sensation reminded me of a time I'd gone to a haunted house and that moment before I looked in the corner. I hadn't really seen the monster there yet, but I knew it was there. I was terrified before I even glimpsed its face.

"Look around you. Really look." Megan squeezed my hand.

I relaxed my eyes and looked past her at my front door, willing myself to see what was hidden. My breathing shuddered as the lines of magic slid into view. Little green sparkles clung to the building. They swam under the wood, undulating and pulsing like a heartbeat. I followed those tendrils out into the yard. They stretched away from my home and out to Point Pleasant.

Tears pricked my eyes. Megan was right. I had been more emotional lately, impatient and impulsive. My confession to Chris had taken longer than it should have. Everyone was giving the same advice, but I couldn't get over my fear, one that grew stronger every night while I slept. When I finally confessed, I'd run away without giving him an opportunity to respond. I hadn't finished reading the latest notebook, even though normally, it would have been a priority. And Bob... Bob was a stubborn jerk sometimes, but he wasn't violent. *Was he under its effect while he was here? Is that why he was so rough with me?* I covered my mouth and stepped back, staring at the green lines reaching toward town. This was too much.

"Look at me," Megan said.

My head turned toward her.

"You should pack a bag. I don't think you should stay here tonight. Do you have someplace safe where you can go?"

I fingered Chris's key in my pocket. He probably hadn't planned on my staying over so soon, but I couldn't think of a place that I felt safer. I nodded.

Megan followed me into the house. Charlie was stalking around the living room, his tail swishing. I scooped him up and carried him with me to the bedroom. Together, Megan and I packed bags for Charlie and me then retreated from the house. Since I was aware of the spell's influence, the inside of my home felt wrong. I could feel the pressure of the spell on the fringes of my thoughts as it tried to dampen my mood.

The Outsider can't have complete control of Grace, though, can it? She called Heather when Bob arrested me. Would it have let her do that? Can she still be saved? I didn't know how I knew, but the answer to that question was yes. My daughter wasn't out of reach.

I followed Megan to her car. Before she got in, she hugged me. "I promise you I'll help you fix this. My ancestors were involved too. You're not alone. But before we can do that, we need to know how far it's spread. And we should try to do that before the Wardens get here. Meet me at my house in the morning, and bring every witch you know."

"How long do we have?"

"Three days." Megan slipped into her car and drove off.

If the stories I had been told about the Wardens were true, that meant I had three days to figure out how to save my daughter.

Can't wait for the next book? You can get book 7, 'Enchantments and the Eerily Ensnared,' here.

In Book 7, During the restoration of Point Pleasant's historic sheriff's center, a decades-old secret is uncovered—literally. A body hidden within the walls pulls Dani Williams into a cold case steeped in betrayal, silence, and long-buried truths.

But this murder isn't just a matter of justice. Dani is convinced the victim's death is connected to the dark force tightening its grip on her daughter, Grace. Solving the mystery may be the only way to stop it.

As Dani digs into the past, the danger becomes frighteningly real. The Wardens of the West have arrived in Point Pleasant, and they aren't interested in explanations—they're looking for Grace. With time running out and the town's secrets unraveling, Dani must uncover the truth before the Wardens take her daughter away forever.

The past and present collide in a race against time, and if Dani fails, she won't just lose the case—she'll lose Grace.

ALSO BY ELOISE EVERHART

A Williams Witch Mystery

Potions and the Pleasantly Poisoned

Tomes and the Tangled Trail

Divinations and the Disappearing Dead

Hexes and the Haunted House

Spells and the Suspiciously Silent

Grimoires and the Ghostly Guest

Enchantments and the Eerily Ensnared

Rituals and the Restless Remains

Charms and the Cursed Coven

A Miller's Magical Mystery

Murder Among the Hives

Murder Between the Stacks

JOIN MY NEWSLETTER

Interested in receiving bonus content like inspiration character art? If so, join our mailing list and receive access to fun things like 'Foresight and the Fateful Ferry,' and character cards. Go on an adventure with Dani and Chris as they journey into Seattle for a fun day out, and things take a dramatic turn when they stumble upon a dead body on the ferry.

ABOUT THE AUTHOR

Eloise Everhart lives in the Pacific Northwest. Her childhood was marked by voracious reading and tabletop roleplaying games, fueling her lifelong passion for storytelling.

By day, she's a dedicated insurance adjuster. It's a career that has honed her sharp eye for detail and developed her inquisitive mind—a skillset she now seamlessly integrates into her cozy mystery writing.

Beyond her storytelling ardor, Eloise is a devoted wife, sharing her home with a menagerie of rescued cats and dogs who have found their furever home in the Everhart household.

ACKNOWLEDGMENTS

I wouldn't have been able to make this book shine without the help of my editors, Rashida Breen and Susie Driver. Without your valuable insights, Rashida, the emotional moments wouldn't hit quite as hard. And Susie, your keen eye really made the prose shine.

To my husband, Nate, for bringing me copious amounts of tea and words of encouragement while I wrote in the evening after my day job. You kept me fueled both physically, and emotionally. Thank you for being my rock.

To my sister, Andrea. I always appreciate your final pass through before I hit publish. You always seem to catch small things that have made it past so many eyes already. You have my gratitude.

And to my best friend, Andrew, who is no longer with us. I will carry you with me, always.

"Come on a journey with me."

www.ingramcontent.com/pod-product-compliance
Lightning Source LLC
LaVergne TN
LVHW050959080826
845145LV00009B/2366

* 9 7 8 1 9 6 2 7 5 9 0 5 2 *